YOU CAN LEAD A HORSE TO WATER . . .

"Hurry, come on. They'll have a posse on us in no time," the first robber complained when they entered the river.

"I can't get this damn horse to lead."

"Bust it in the ass." The first rider turned around, and his jaw sagged at the sight of Slocum as he stepped out from behind the cottonwood trunk.

"Shuck them guns. Get them hands high or die, boys!"

"Who the fuck are you?" The outlaw's exhale was more of a shudder.

"The man stopping you. Now get them hands up or die, boys. I won't mess with you." Slocum looked down the barrel of the Winchester, ready to squeeze the trigger at the first sign of any resistance.

"Oh, praise the Lord," the banker said and promptly fell off the horse into the muddy water. His arms flailed the water like a paddle boat . . .

JAKE LOGAN

SLOCUM AND THE KETCHEM GANG

JOVE BOOKS, NEW YORK

SLOCUM AND THE KETCHEM GANG

A Jove Book / published by arrangement with
the author

PRINTING HISTORY
Jove edition / November 1999

All rights reserved.
Copyright © 1999 by Penguin Putnam Inc.
This book may not be reproduced in whole or in part,
by mimeograph or any other means, without permission.
For information address: The Berkley Publishing Group,
a division of Penguin Putnam Inc.,
375 Hudson Street, New York, New York 10014.

The Penguin Putnam Inc. World Wide Web site address is
http://www.penguinputnam.com

ISBN: 0-515-12686-1

A JOVE BOOK®
Jove Books are published by The Berkley Publishing Group,
a division of Penguin Putnam Inc.,
375 Hudson Street, New York, New York 10014.
JOVE and the "J" design
are trademarks belonging to Penguin Putnam Inc.

PRINTED IN THE UNITED STATES OF AMERICA

10 9 8 7 6 5 4 3 2 1

1

He tried to focus his eyes, blinded by the bright Kansas sunshine when he stepped out of the Alhambra Saloon onto the porch. Across the railroad tracks and headed toward him rode a familiar figure on a stout line-back yellow horse. It was a big man dressed in a long canvas coat and Boss of the Plains hat, the same sumbitch who owed him two hundred dollars, John Rhodes.

Slocum rubbed his whisker-bristled mouth with his left hand, and considered his good fortune. Rhodes had no idea who was standing there in dust-floured clothing, a fresh arrival in the Queen City of Dodge. Why, Slocum had only been there long enough to down two stiff drinks inside the Alhambra. The rye whiskey had cut a little of the three months' accumulation of trail dust from his throat.

"Afternoon," Slocum offered.

"Yeah, good evening," Rhodes said and stepped down, paying no attention to Slocum as he hitched his horse. He methodically wrapped the reins on the rack, then looked up mildly.

His eyelids flew open at his discovery. "That you, Slocum?"

"Ain't his brother. How about my money?" He held out his palm toward the man.

"Why—why—I ain't got it."

Slocum nodded toward Rhodes's middle. "Dig in that money belt around that waist of yours and get it out."

"I swear I've been concerned about you and that money I owe you, but right now—"

"The right now part is dig out the money you owe me." Slocum's eyes narrowed to slits as the rage inside his chest began to seethe. Rhodes had skipped out on him in San Antonio after promising to pay him. He would be at the cantina at dark with it, he'd said. He'd forgotten to say which day at dark, because Slocum had waited until midnight, then gone looking for him and learned he'd ridden out of town in mid-afternoon.

"Can't do that," Rhodes now said. "This ain't my money."

"Too damn bad. But you ain't coming up on this porch unless you pay me."

Rhodes scratched at his ear and then made a pained face. "I don't have the money right now."

"You heard me, dig it out."

"I told you—"

Filled with contempt, Slocum left the porch in a bound, and his right fist smashed into Rhodes's face and sent him sprawling on his butt beside the horse. He'd had enough of this confidence man's denials and lies. He wanted his money and wasn't taking no for an answer.

"You've got to listen, Slocum." Rhodes held out his hands to ward off any more blows as he crawfished away on his butt to escape Slocum's wrath.

"I'm only listening to how you are going to pay me." Then Slocum stopped, frowned, and looked around. Something was happening at the Livestock and Merchants Exchange Bank three doors down the street, and he didn't like the looks of it. A boy of perhaps eighteen outside the front door held three horses by the reins and was looking around like a wild man.

Then shots sounded from inside the bank, and Slocum

realized a robbery was in progress. He jerked the Winchester out of Rhodes's scabbard, which drew an audible scream of protest from the cattle buyer still on his butt.

The horse handler by this time had his own pistol out, and began shooting wildly at everyone left on Front Street. Slocum took aim and dropped him, the horses set free when he slumped to the street. They shied and crossed the tracks about the time the other two robbers rushed out with the bank loot in their hands.

"Get your hands up!" Slocum shouted.

For his effort, he drew some whistling hot lead that went by close enough. Then he dropped down to his knees, using the horse for protection. His cheek pressed to the stock, he took aim and squeezed off a round.

His shot tugged at one robber's sleeve. The two bandits reconsidered, then headed back inside the bank, grumbling about where in the hell their horses had gone.

"Good shot. I'll cover the back exit," a man in a black frock coat said, out of breath, and he headed between the Alhambra and the mercantile for the alley in back. "Drop them if they bust out."

Slocum nodded to the lawman. By this time Rhodes had managed to crawl past his horse and press himself under the stoop of the boardwalk.

"It's about over. You can pay me now." Slocum never looked in his direction. "Good rifle you got here."

"You're crazy! Out there and taking a chance on getting your ass shot off!" Rhodes declared in disbelief.

"I'm more worried about you paying me. They steal all that money from the bank, you won't be able to borrow any to pay me off."

"Borrow any—why, I can't do that." The clatter of broken glass forced Slocum to use the buckskin horse for cover.

"Keep your head down," he said over his shoulder to Rhodes. "One of them just broke a pane out of the bank's front window."

"Hey, we've got this banker here, and if you don't get

us some fresh horses and a way out of here, he's dead!'' the robber called. "Do you hear me?''

No one answered. Slocum had no authority. He glanced around for the law. Another man in a black frock coat nodded at him from the saloon porch, then sent a boy after horses.

"Hold up, I've sent for horses,'' the lawman shouted.

Then the man joined Slocum at the horse and looked warily at the bank's front. "Name's Earp. Morgan Earp. You've done real well here, but I'd say if we want to see Mr. Peabody stay alive, we better back down and let them two ride out.''

"Slocum's my name. You're the law. I'm just a citizen.'' He let the rifle down, unloaded the chamber, and then shoved it back in the scabbard.

"You did good. My brother's in the alley and more help's coming.'' Morgan didn't take his eyes off the bank, a long barrel Colt in his fist, ready for action.

"Rhodes, you ready to pay me?'' Slocum asked over his shoulder.

"I guess. It ain't my money, but . . .''

Slocum looked in disgust at the cattle buyer seated on his butt. He wanted to chuckle at the sight of the man as Rhodes busily dug the paper money out of his money belt. Slocum didn't give a gawdamn whose money Rhodes carried, so long as he was paid. Ought to charge the lying no-account interest on it too.

"Here comes the boy with the horses,'' Morgan said, and stepped out in the street.

"Get another horse,'' the robber shouted. "We're taking Peabody to the river with us.''

Earp cursed, then with a black scowl sent the boy back for another mount. Rhodes handed the money to Slocum without ever rising up from his place on the ground. Slocum wadded it up and jammed it in his front pocket.

The man frowned in disbelief. "You never counted it.''

"I didn't need to. If you've shorted me, I'll beat it out

of your hide. Excuse me, I need to borrow your horse for thirty minutes.''

"Where you going?" Earp asked with a frown.

"To see a man about a dog."

"When will I get my horse back?" Rhodes whined.

"In about thirty minutes." Slocum checked the cinch, threw up the reins, and then swung aboard. He loped the dun west past the railroad station, rounded it, crossed the tracks, and headed south for the river at a high lope.

Concealed behind a cottonwood on the south bank in the warm sunshine, Slocum waited for the robbers. The lazy reddish-brown Arkansas River stretched a hundred yards wide before him, dazzling in the bright solar rays.

A wagon pulled by four tall cotton mules came from the south. Slocum looked towards Dodge for any sign of the outlaws. Then he stepped out and waved the wagon down. An attractive full-figured woman in her mid-thirties with flaming red hair reined in the mules.

"Outlaws coming this way fast," Slocum said. "Swing out of the way. There may be shooting, ma'am."

"Thank you, sir," she said, and rose to shout to the youth herding some colts behind her. "We've got to get out of the way."

The boy nodded and sent the ponies to the right. She expertly wheeled the mules aside. Satisfied they would be out of the line of fire, Slocum turned his attention back to the road out of Dodge. Soon he could hear the drum of hooves and smiled to himself; they were coming his way.

There were three riders—two robbers, in front, one leading a wide-eyed man in a starched white shirt on the last horse. Slocum planned to let them get over halfway across the Arkansas before he stopped them.

"Hurry, come on. They'll have a posse on us in no time," the first robber complained when they entered the river.

"I can't get this damn horse to lead."

"Bust it in the ass." The first rider turned around, and

his jaw sagged at the sight of Slocum as he stepped out from behind the cottonwood trunk.

"Shuck them guns. Get them hands high or die, boys!"

"Who the fuck are you?" The outlaw's exhale was more of a shudder.

"The man stopping you. Now get them hands up or die, boys. I won't mess with you." Slocum looked down the barrel of the Winchester, ready to squeeze the trigger at the first sign of any resistance.

"Oh, praise the Lord," the banker said, and promptly fell off the horse into the muddy water. With his arms flailing the water like a paddle boat, he soon discovered to his chagrin that the water was only inches deep. Bubbling and sputtering, he stood up in dejected shock; the muddy water dripped from his clothing. The shirt was no longer white, but a dingy rust brown.

Both outlaws sat their horses, their hands high in the air. Slocum kept the rifle on them. He could see the black hats and frock coats of the town's law men coming on their back-trail.

"Whoa!" Morgan Earp shouted to the horse he rode, then seeing that Slocum had the robbers, turned his mount off into the river.

"You're a handy man, Slocum," he said, riding up to disarm the pair. "You all right, Mr. Peabody?" Earp asked the wet banker, who had waded out and stood looking dejected on the bank.

"Me? I'm fine. Thanks to that man!" He pointed toward Slocum.

"His name's Slocum," Earp said. "You boys should have teethed yourself on this bank-robbing business in another town." He handcuffed each man's hands behind him, then herded them out of the river. Two other deputies took charge of the pair.

Slocum put the Winchester back, helped Peabody get on his horse, then mounted up and started for town. Then remembering, he looked around for the attractive redhead driving the mules, but didn't see any sign of her. She and that boy hadn't gotten hurt, at least.

"What business you in, Mr. Slocum?" Morgan asked, riding beside him.

"Cattle driving. Brought a herd up from down in the south Brazos country."

"I appreciate your help today," Earp said.

"I appreciate him enough that I'm paying him a two-hundred-fifty-dollar reward," Peabody said, sitting the horse in a round-butted fashion.

"He deserves it," Earp agreed. "Welcome to Dodge City, Mr. Slocum."

"Slocum's fine," he said. "And I'm proud to be here."

He considered the long row of buildings and establishments that faced the railroad yards and the pens full of bellowing cattle being loaded or waiting to be loaded. He was glad to be there with his pockets full of new money. Not to mention what Sam Cantrel owed him for the cattle drive.

"Buy you a drink later," Earp said, and reined his horse east. Slocum gave the lawman a wave and turned back to Peabody.

"Come over to the bank. I'm paying you that reward right now," the banker said with a nod of his head.

"I'll be right over there. I see the man owns this horse and he looks impatient for me to return him." Slocum also noted the crowd of onlookers gathered at the front porch of the bank. A man under a celluloid visor came running out to help his boss with his horse.

"It will be waiting for you," Peabody said, standing on the ground, looking very disheveled in his muddy shirt, with his black hair standing peaked in the wind.

"Guess you got them?" Rhodes asked with a scowl, and took the reins when Slocum dismounted.

"Yes, we did."

"Slocum—I'll get even with you over this," Rhodes said, then mounted and started off in a huff.

"Even for what?" Slocum blinked his eyes after the man.

Rhodes had threatened him. It didn't make much sense, but Rhodes was mad as a wet hen for having to pay Slocum the money he'd owed him for over two years.

"Never mind," Rhodes said without turning.

Slocum cast a hard look at the man's back. He sucked on his left rear molar—it damn sure meant *something*. From behind, he could hear that banker Peabody calling to him. He turned on his heels and headed for the crowd as a flash from a photographer went off and a white puff of smoke rose in the air.

They were taking pictures of the dead robber propped up on two wide boards against the hitch rail. Slocum shook his head in disbelief. How morbid could the newspapers get?

"My name's Arnold Stipes of the *Kansas City Herald*. Could I have your name, sir?" a young, eager-faced man asked with a pencil and pad in hand.

"Slocum."

"First or last?"

"J. Slocum."

"Thanks. Good. Where do you live, sir?"

"Texas."

"You're a cattle drover?" The young man's green eyes were afire with eagerness.

"Yes. Brought a herd up today."

"You know any of these outlaws?"

"No. Never saw them before."

"They say you stopped the whole robbery single-handed."

Slocum shook his head in reply to the reporter. Then the bank teller began to pull on Slocum's sleeve. "Mr. Peabody wants you to come inside and collect your reward."

"Reward?" the reporter shouted.

"Mr. Peabody wants to express his appreciation to Mr. Slocum for stopping the robbery and saving the bank's money."

"How much of a reward?"

"Two hundred fifty dollars."

"That's a lot of money. What will you be doing with that much money?" the eager young reporter asked from close beside Slocum as they went inside the bank's interior.

"Go back to Texas and make another drive, I guess."

Pencil poised, Stipes shouldered his way through the crowd to keep up with Slocum. The energy and poise of the young man amused Slocum when he stopped at the wooden fence that separated the bank lobby from the outer portion.

"Come on back," Peabody said, waving to him; he was already dressed in a fresh starched shirt and adjusting an ascot knot in his tie. "My britches are still wet, but that won't matter. I'm alive thanks to you."

"Did you know any of the Ketchem gang?" the reporter asked.

"That's who they were?" Slocum asked, and shook the banker's hand.

"Arlie is the dead one out front. Bret and Hailey Ketchem are the other two. They're wanted all over. Bet there's several more rewards on them too."

Slocum nodded. He really didn't appreciate all the fuss this newsman was making out of nothing. And he didn't need the Abbott brothers reading the Kansas City newspaper and learning about his business and whereabouts. The Abbotts were two bounty hunters hired by a rich man out of Fort Scott, Kansas, to stay on his tracks.

"Lennie, bring me the money for Mr. Slocum," Peabody said.

"Did you recover all the loot?" Stipes asked the banker.

"Yes, every dime of it."

"How much did they take?"

"We aren't certain. We're still counting it, but it was a substantial amount and thanks to Slocum here, the money is safely back." Peabody took the gold coins from the teller and began to count them out. "I trust you like coins."

Slocum nodded.

"What are you going to do next?" Stipes asked Slocum.

"Go talk to a few cattle buyers, then go back to the herd."

"Not going to celebrate?"

"Do that after I get the herd sold."

"I guess so. Sure nice to meet you, Slocum." Stipes changed hands with his pencil and shook Slocum's hand.

"I can ever help you, Slocum, call on me," Peabody announced with his chest stuck out.

Slocum nodded thanks and headed for the door. His bay was up the street at the stables; he did need to see a few buyers, feel out the market, and get back to the herd.

Outside in the sunlight, he rubbed his whisker-bristled upper lip on the side of his hand. This was where he'd been an hour or so earlier. Never could tell what would turn up next in Dodge. He headed for the Cattlemen's Exchange on the corner. He pushed in the frosted-glass front door and stood on the tiled floor of the lobby. A giant longhorn steer's head hung over the hallway entrance that led back to the various commission companies. Slocum went to Laddie and Simon's office. The door was open, and he removed his high-crown hat and stepped inside.

"Slocum, you back already?" the full-faced man at the desk asked.

"Back again, O'Malley, and have some fat cattle. Where are the bosses?" he asked, looking into the open doors at the empty offices.

"Out looking at cattle. Where are you located at?"

"Holding about ten miles south. Guess you could tell one of them to come look and make a bid."

"I don't know. . . ." The man acted pained.

"What's wrong?"

"This market isn't much good and they aren't buying many steers. You got much she-stuff?"

"She-stuff?" Slocum shook his head.

"Yeah, they're shipping herds to Montana now. Got some real grass up there and a real good market for cows and heifers."

"What are steers bringing in, O'Malley?"

"Six cents a pound, if you can find a buyer."

"Why, that won't pay my help for the drive."

"I can't help the market, Slocum."

"I know," Slocum said grimly. Maybe Rhodes's two hundred and the banker's reward would be his only profit on this trip, and he might even have to use it all to settle his accounts. Still, he couldn't believe from spring to fall the market had gone that sour. Something was wrong here. Why, Sam Cantrel would pay six cents a pound on the Brazos.

"Tell them to ride out and see my cattle," Slocum said to the man.

"I will, but it won't help the market any."

"What are other folks doing?"

"Going to winter them over and hope for better prices in the spring."

Thanks," Slocum said. With the man's advice under consideration, he walked out the door. Maybe Vince Strong had better news than that.

He headed down the hallway until he reached Strong's office. He tried the door and found it locked. Which was strange since it was the middle of the week.

"Looking for Mr. Strong?" a young man under a green celluloid visor asked, leaning out the door of an adjoining office.

"Yes, I was."

"He's left town, they say."

"Oh?"

The young man looked up and down the hall to be certain they were alone. "He ran off."

"Any reason?"

"Low cattle market. Got caught with several herds he paid too much for. Owes a sizeable sum of money. . . ." The man looked around again, then spoke lower. "Ran off with one of Earp's girls too."

"Which Earp?"

"Wyatt."

"Thanks." Slocum recalled Wyatt from years before down in the Indian Nation. No doubt Wyatt would be angry, and as pompous as ever. For a moment, Slocum felt more depressed over the shape of the cattle market than anything else. What should he do next? Obviously O'Malley had not lied to him, not even shaded the truth. Vince Strong leaving Dodge owing others money didn't sound right, but sometimes a shapely skirt could change a man's character. Slocum figured he better get back to the herd.

2

Hailey Ketchem stood on the bunk so he could view the alley behind the jail through the barred windows. Piles of trash littered the ground, and a few cur dogs growled over some scraps beneath him. Nothing else was in sight. This wasn't his first stay in a cell, but he never liked them no matter how short the visits.

"Who was that bastard got us?" he asked his brother Bret over his shoulder.

"Called him Slocum."

Hailey never turned back, keeping his gaze on the littered space behind the jail. He ever got the sumbitch in his sights, Slocum was dead. The name didn't mean a thing to him— another Texas drover, he supposed. Bastard like that needed his balls cut off for putting himself in a place where he didn't belong. A fly droned in Hailey's ear; he waved it away, then reached down and scratched a deep itch in his privates, still upset at this fella Slocum for barging in. Otherwise, they'd have gotten slick away.

"Ma's going to be mad," Bret said.

"About Arlie getting hisself kilt?"

"You know we're going to be blamed for it."

"Hell, we didn't know that Slocum was going to be there."

"She'll still be pissed about it. Arlie was her pet."

"I'm pissed we got ourselves caught. It don't do me no good to be pissed to be in this gawdamn jail, does it?"

"I guess not." Bret mopped his sweaty face with his kerchief. "Hotter'n hell in here."

"We ain't going to be here long."

"Huh?"

"Hush up." Hailey lowered his voice. "I said we ain't going to be here long."

"How the fuck we getting out of here?"

"Start watching for a chance. They'll slip up and we'll get a chance. You be ready to run for it."

"Arlie's dead. Oh, damn, I'd like to—"

"We'll get that Slocum. You can bet your boots we'll get his ass when we get out. Stop worrying about Arlie and start figuring how we're getting out of here."

"You can't pry them bars loose, can you?"

Hailey tried them, then shook his head. "They're in there too damn good."

"I hate that boy got hisself kilt," Bret moaned.

Hailey wished his brother would shut up about the damn death. The kid was dead and they couldn't do a thing about it. So the old woman would be pissed off. He couldn't help that, but they needed out of jail bad. The Dodge bank job wasn't that big of a charge, but the one in Wichita where they'd shot several stupid people that got in the way would get them hung. No one ever hung a simple bank robber but vigilantes, and the two of them were under the protection of the Earps in this city jail. All they could get were a couple years in the Kansas pen. Hailey had no intention of ever serving that time at hard labor. Had to be a way to spring them out of this cow town brig. He dropped down to the bunk. There had to be a way out.

The food they were served tasted like slop to Hailey. Some dried-up, over-cooked pancakes for breakfast with a little molasses. If he hadn't been starved to death, he'd have thrown the shit right in the jailer's face.

One lawman with a shotgun backed the prisoner who served them their food. He kept one hammer cocked, and brought it up with every intention of using it when the prisoner handed them the plates. Hailey mentally measured the swing of the iron-barred door; the gun-toting watchdog stayed clear of its possible path.

If ever a guard was in the way, Hailey could shove the door aside and whip down the barrel and wrestle it away from him in an instant. That would be his plan—jam him with the door, grab the gun. But he better not worry Bret with his plan. From his own experience, he knew Bret would only fret about how it would work. Damn wonder they'd managed to successfully hold up over a dozen banks and stage untold individual robberies.

They'd miss Arlie. Bad deal. That redheaded whore Joetta up in Salinia would miss him too. Dumb kid sent her his money all the time. And everyone knew she went right on screwing her customers. What did he think she was going to do, living and working in a damn whore house? Why, she blew his money like she did her own. Saying she was saving them a damn nest egg—that whore was lying like a bitch.

"You got a plan?" Bret asked under his breath, slumped over, sitting on the other bunk, looking overheated.

"I'll have one in a day or so."

"Won't be the same without the kid."

"Can't bring him back. We'll even the score with this Slocum."

"We got to—Ma won't like it."

Hailey looked at the ceiling for help. Who gave a shit what she liked and disliked? Damn, they weren't little kids heisting travelers' pants pockets while she got them in her bed. Soon as she got to bucking an old boy on the mattress, he and Bret crawled in the room, robbed the fella's pants, and got away. Hailey could remember many times hearing her moan and groan and a customer panting like a wind-broke horse and grunting like an old hog the whole time he poked her. The bed ropes would be creaking, and a musky smell would be in the air that he found out years later came from the lather that a man's rod made inside a woman. Afterward, the men usually cursed and swore that they'd been robbed, but she'd hustle them out the door. When it was safe, the two boys returned and gave her all the money.

He could remember her whipping him with a hickory switch for holding out ten cents from her. She'd stripped his overalls down, held him up by one arm, and beaten his bare ass bloody with the stick until he'd admitted he had the dime.

How she ever knew he had secreted that coin, he never found out. But she did, and though he tried his eight-year-old damnedest not to tell her the whole time, he ended up hurting so much from her whipping that he began to pee on their feet. He couldn't help it. Then she whipped him for doing that.

He was so sore he never slept at all that night. The bed-cover stuck to his bleeding backside. Bret took him to the horse tank behind McGruder's barn and washed him off. A woman named Aunt Sally gave Bret some homemade salve to put on it. Hailey came close to peeing in his pants when his brother doctored him with the stuff. Never again did he try to steal any of the loot—he'd learned his lesson.

He could remember her hugging him the next evening, saying she was sorry she'd hurt him, all those sissy things, like she loved him and had done it for his own good. Cold chills ran up his spine at the memory of the searing pain.

"We're in deep this time," Bret said, and brought Hailey back to the present.

"Hell, you said that in Missouri."

"Damn, we was—"

"Stop worrying. We ain't staying in this place long. Trust me."

"I sure liked that bay horse I rode in here on. Sam was a damn good pony."

"Forget him. That Earp called Wyatt's got him already. Heard them talking out in the office first thing today about that blood bay. Rode him over someplace, said he had a running walk. That's Sam. You've seen the last of that one."

"Sumbitch, I want to kill that Slocum."

Hailey rose and went to the front of the cell; he pressed his forehead to the cool bars. It felt good. If he only had more to lean against.

"You got company, boys," the turnkey shouted. Earlier they'd marched all the drunks out for court, so the cells were empty save for a breed in the end cell who never said two words.

Hailey blinked at the white-bearded man with the bible who held a stovepipe hat in his hand. Ma had sent Luther, the old man she lived with.

"You can sit on the outside of the cell and talk to them, preacher," the turnkey said. "But let me warn you, they need more than any hellfire-and-brimstone message."

"Bless you, son," the old man said in a gravelly voice to the jailer.

"I bring a message from your mother, Inabella," the man said, looking at Hailey out of his rheumy eyes.

Inabella? Shitfire, her name was Ruby. What kind of crap was Luther saying? Ruby Marsha Ketchem had never known a church—nor a preacher either unless he had a hard-on.

"How we getting out of here?" Hailey hissed.

"I'm here to read the Good Book." The man scraped the wooden chair across the stone floor to get closer to the bars.

"What the hell's he talking about—"

Hailey cut Bret's words off with a wave of his hand, and looked hard as the old man opened the worn, tattered bible.

"The Lord—" the man began in a loud voice, and turned the book so Hailey could read the note.

AFTER MIDNIGHT.

"May he save your souls. Let me look here for a good verse that should prepare you for your escape to the Lord. Amen."

"Amen," Hailey said. He met the man's gaze and knew that Ma had sent him to give them the word. She would break them out before daylight.

In a monotone, the man began to read, and Hailey waved Bret in close. "Start amen-ing this."

For a moment his brother half jerked away, but seeing the seriousness in Hailey's face, he joined in like a Baptist.

"Hallelujah!"

"Praise the Lord!" And the old man rambled on with his scriptures.

"Yes, and dear Jesus."

"I can see, my sons, that your dear mother's prayers have been answered and you have returned to the flock. Let us pray."

"Amen."

Hailey frowned at Bret. Not time for that yet—he ain't said the prayer. But maybe Bret knew more about prayers than *he* did. When they were in their teens and living in Springfield, Missouri, Bret used to take out this preacher's daughter. He would have to attend prayer meetings with her. Then he could walk her home, which included a quick visit to Thomas Whitten's horse barn.

In the tack room, which smelled of saddle soap, Barbara Cockrane would hoist up her skirt and petticoats faster than any woman he ever knew. She would bend over and accept them one at a time from behind. She usually wanted to kiss Hailey too when they finished. Her mouth tasted like some kind of perfumed soap. Once while he was giving it to her, he reached around front to discover she had no pubic hair. He decided she must be a lot younger than Bret thought.

Then in a few months she upped and married a thirty-five-year-old man, a deacon in the church, Bret said.

Three months later, Hailey was on the prowl for things to filch. Headed down an alley, he spotted Barbara in her backyard through a knothole in the board fence. She was all alone in a thin shift that the wind caused to wrap around her swollen stomach.

He hissed at her, and she came to the fence acting like he wasn't there.

"Hey, let me in, Barb."

"I can't," she hissed, standing close to his place. "I'm married."

"Hey, Bret really was upset you married that fella."

"I had to." She gave him an impatient look.

"Why?"

"I had to. I was with child," she said in a hushed whisper.

"Oh."

"Go away."

"Is he home?"

"Nope, but the neighbors might talk."

"What if you open the gate and I crawled on my belly to that shed and you opened the door and we go in there. I've sure missed you." Hailey glanced up and down the alley. He was getting hard thinking about her butt. What could he do to convince her? He knew she wanted it—he could tell.

"I don't know," she said.

"Say, think about all the good times we had in the tack room."

"Oh, that's why I am married," she said, sounding disappointed.

"Well, I can't hurt you talking," he said. If she ever went inside the shed with him, he knew he would have his way. His pants began to fill with his stiffening dick at the notion of having her smooth butt again.

"You must get very low," she finally said in a small voice.

"They'll never see me." He dried his sweaty hands on the front of his pants and stepped to the gate. When she opened it, he was on the ground like a cat, and used his elbows to keep low along the fence until he reached the shed and she opened the door.

Inside, the building smelled of nicotine and bat manure. Cobwebs draped down from the rafters. Things were stacked inside that folks used in their gardens. A soft light came in through the dusty single windowpane. He could smell her soapy smell, and hugged her, feeling the bulge of her baby between them.

"Your man got a big one?" he asked.

She shook her head and looked about to cry.

"He don't?"

"It's limp. He can't get it in me," she said, sounding so desperate about the man's state that he even felt sorry for her and her husband.

"Wish I could help," he said in her ear. Her arms went around him and hugged him closer.

"So do I."

"Guess you couldn't bend over—"

"Oh yes, I could," she said, and a smile spread over her sweaty red face. "But you must be fast."

"I'll try."

She hugged him again, then kissed his mouth. "Not too fast, though."

"I won't be." His breath drained out of him and his erection grew harder.

She bent over, then threw the shift over her back. In the dull light he ran his hands over the smooth skin of her double mounds, and then reached into his fly and curled a finger around his shaft. Filled with excitement, he stepped up behind her. She gave a sharp cry at his entry, and he began to pump it to her.

Faster and faster, the odor of their lather came to him above the smell of the shed's contents, mingled with her perfume. He felt her begin to contract around him. Both of them grew short of breath, and he had her hips in his hands as he pounded away.

Then she cried out and strained. Strained so hard he went

off inside her and he was forced to catch himself on the nearby table. The leg gave way and they both tumbled to the ground dazed, and things began to shower down on them. Empty berry cups and wicker baskets, a small shovel, and two rake handles.

"Oh," she said, unshaken, but detached from him by the fall. Her hands sought his face, and she climbed over everything and began to kiss him.

"You are so wonderful, Hailey Ketchem." He could taste her lavender soap again and that made his hard-on go away.

She kept alternating between kissing him and saying how much she liked him. He recovered his erection again, and amid the boxes and tools her hand found it and she gave a cry at her discovery. Her fist began to pump it; he sat halfway up amid the rubbish. His legs hung over two tomato crates, and this lavender-stinking girl was jacking him off. The friction of her palm soon had him rock-hard.

"Be still," she said, gathering her shift before he could do anything. She rose up, stepped over the rakes' handles, held up her silky shift, and settled herself on his rod. In a minute she began to buck up and down on him. He wondered if she had grown any pubic hair. In the shed's dim light he couldn't tell. Up and down she went as if to crush him into the dirt floor, his back and shoulders hung up on a wooden box, until at last she gave a loud sigh and settled down on him.

"You must come back next week," she said, her face flushed with excitement.

"Your husband?"

She rose astraddle him, showing him her exposed swollen bare belly, but in the shadows he still couldn't tell if she had any hair or not. At last he scrambled to his feet and she hugged him. His curiosity was so great, he used the opportunity to reach down and check her. His fingers slid over the round of her protruding stomach, and soon he felt the wet slash. Nothing but bare skin.

"Oh, you want to do it again?" she asked, and swept the wet hair back from her face.

"No, I have to go to work," he lied.

Now Hailey stood with his forehead pressed to the cell bars, and stared at the shaft of afternoon sunlight that shone in a frame on the corridor floor through the open door to the marshal's office. It had been a long time since he'd screwed Barbara in the garden shed.

3

Slocum swirled the coffee in his cup. A hint of smoke from the sagebrush and cow-chip fire swept by his nose on the restless wind. The crew was gathered and the cowboys sat about on the ground waiting for his word on their future.

"This cattle market has fallen lower than a whale's belly," he began. "Best price I heard of in town was six cents a pound. That ain't even worth considering. The man won't—hell, Cantrel *can't* take that for them. Means we need to winter them up here, I imagine. I know that's disappointing to some of you that got wives and ranches back home to worry about. But all of us don't need to stay over. It won't take everyone to winter the herd. The rest of you can collect your pay when Cantrel gets here and ride home is all I know."

"When's them that's going home going to get paid?" Curly Bob asked.

"The man will be here in a few days. We made better time than I thought. He's due in here Monday." Slocum looked at the cook, Estancho, who kept meticulous records.

"This is Friday," the swarthy-faced man in the soiled apron offered.

"Thanks. Give me an account of those who can stay with the herd," Slocum told the men.

Several hands went up. Enough, he figured. "The rest of you can plan on heading back or raising hell after he pays you off Monday."

"You mean we got to set out here all weekend long?" Joe Dale Whitacker asked, pained. "And them pretty ladies in there so anxious to climb on my barber pole?"

Slocum grinned at the young man. "They'll wait for it."

"We all got to stay with the herd?" Joe Dale asked.

"We can split in half," Slocum agreed. "Half can go to town, the other half need to stay and keep them bunched. When the first ones come back, then someone else can go in."

The seated cowboys waved their hats and hooted at his offer.

"That sounds settled. I can loan anyone needs it ten bucks a man against his pay."

"I want that loan." Others joined in the chorus, and Slocum was soon doling out money to the boys.

The conversation over, and with four of the cowhands sent back to tend the herd spread out across the grassland, Slocum watched the other half of the outfit saddle up and head for Dodge. There would be some sore heads in the morning and some sore peckers too. "Dodge, watch out," he thought. "The real ones are going to taste your wine, women, and song."

"What will you do, Señor?" the cook asked, busy working down his mound of snowy sourdough in the great granite dish.

"Get Cantrel to hire someone to ramrod the outfit and I'll move on."

"I don't blame you, Señor. It gets *mucho* gawdamn cold up here in the winter."

"Too cold for you, Estancho?"

"Oh, man, I thought I would freeze my balls off once I was up here in November and winter wasn't even here yet. I couldn't get back to Texas fast enough."

"I kind of figured I'd ride up to Ogallala and see the sights," Slocum said absently.

"Where would you go from there?"

"Maybe Fort Laramie. Want to go along?"

The man scowled and then shrugged. "I never seen that country."

"Be different. We still have a couple of months before the north wind blows down."

"Whew, I sure don't want to be here then."

Slocum agreed, and went to refill his tin coffee cup. Using his kerchief to protect his hand, he poured coffee in the mug, then hung the pot back on the S hook. He studied the distant forms of the steers. Why couldn't it have been easy—load them on the train cars, collect the money, and be gone, and he'd have no more obligation. That would have been too damn easy.

One thing for certain, he couldn't sit with the cattle all winter. Some bounty hunter or the Abbott brothers would ride up there before long. Their presence on his backtrail kept him sugar-footing around.

"Hey, banker, you hungry?" Estancho asked, breaking into his thoughts about the sour turn of events.

Slocum grinned back at the man's teasing ways. He was lucky he had any money to loan. Running into Rhodes and collecting the banker's reward had made him a little heavy in the pockets.

"Not hungry. I may ride out and circle the herd before dark."

"Won't be many to feed tonight then." The cook shook his head, wiped his hands on the tail of his apron, and went to stoke up his fires.

Slocum checked the sun in the western sky. It was still a few hours till sundown. Days were getting shorter, but it was still late August, and a hot breath of Kansas prairie wind swept over his face when he swung up on the blue roan. He shrugged his stiff shoulders, then booted the roan into a long jog. Better go see about his wards—three thousand damn near worthless steers.

He had made a pass to the west of them when he spotted a wagon coming out of the south. The yellow canvas on the bows shone in the blazing sun and two teams of mules were lugging it along. Must be another cow outfit arriving from Texas. Out of curiosity he set out towards it. Maybe he knew them.

He drew near, then recognized the woman with the flaming red hair who stood up and reined in the mules. A small string of young horses trailed the outfit, and the boy in his teens in overalls and a floppy hat drove them.

"Afternoon again," Slocum said, removing his hat for her.

"Afternoon yourself," she said, looking a little peeved at him.

"Any trouble, Ma?" the boy asked, reining in his horse short of Slocum. With a defensive set to his eyes, he looked Slocum over with suspicion.

"I can handle it, Jeremy," she said to the boy. His skin was a dark brown from the sun, and all he wore were the tattered overalls. His dusty bare feet hung below the faded worn saddle blanket he rode.

A handsome woman with a fair complexion, she wore a stained, wide-brimmed straw hat that shaded her sharp green eyes and slender nose. It was her mouth that fascinated Slocum the most. The wide full lips looked like feather pillows and needed to be kissed.

"My name's Slocum, ma'am."

"Yes, we met earlier as I recall. Glendora Brown. This is my boy, Jeremy. Can I go around Dodge City by going this way?" She looked past him with some impatience.

The mules blew wearily and bobbed their heads. Lathered under the collars, they appeared gaunt from their journey. Her whole rig showed plenty of wear. The harness bore hasty repairs, and patches of the torn canvas cover flapped in the persistent wind. But Glendora Brown looked out of place, even with canvas pants showing under her skirt hem—too pretty a woman for the plight she looked to be in.

"Head a little west and cross the river there," he said.

"Good. Hear that, Jeremy?" she asked.

"Yes ma'am."

"We'll be moving on then," she said, taking up the reins and sounding impatient to be on her way.

"I could show you the best crossing," he offered, wishing he'd taken a bath and cleaned up in town, instead of downing those drinks and tending to the Earps' business.

"I think we can find our way." She started to undo the wagon's brake with a dusty boot.

"Going around Dodge?"

"Yes, I want nothing to do with that place." She sounded affronted he would even ask. "I may need some supplies from there, but we'll bypass it. This is the way to Ogallala?"

"Ogallala?" he asked, anxious to extend his time with her. He wanted to know more about such a beautiful woman who was out on the prairie with only a boy of perhaps thirteen. "Yes, but it's a long ways up there."

"My husband is there waiting for us," she said, and clucked to the mules. He drew back the roan, nodded, and wished her a good day. The boy avoided looking at him in passing, herding the young horses along after the wagon.

Slocum removed his Boss of the Plains hat and scratched the top of his head. You met all kinds out on the prairie, but that voluptuous redhead had flat ignored his every effort to know her better. Damn, maybe he needed more than a bath, shave, and set of clean clothes. He watched the wagon rattle off to the north. Then he set the roan eastward. That kind of a good-looking woman made his empty stomach roil at the very notion of what she'd be like in a feather bed.

He looked back again, still not believing how easily she had dismissed him. She was having no part of the Queen City of cow towns either. She and that boy of hers, who was baked as dark as Estancho's normal color, were going

north to find her husband. He'd bet that fella was waiting
for her on some homestead with a big hard-on. How a man
could leave something that special to homestead out on the
prairie alone was beyond him.

Oh, well, she had a man—up in Nebraska. He'd never
learned the exact location either. In fact, there wasn't much
he *did* know about the pair. He glanced over his shoulder
at the distant tottering oval top of the wagon. Whew, she
sure was a looker. He booted the roan into a long lope.
Maybe some of Estancho's food would settle his guts, but
he doubted it.

After supper, he considered going into Dodge and checking on his revelers. But the fatigue of the day settled in and
instead, he decided they were all big enough to take care of
themselves; he turned into his blankets at some distance
from the camp after discussing the details of the night herding with the boys left to stand guard.

The cattle were settled and the sky clear of any brooding
thunderstorms, and he soon found sleep. But in his slumber,
the redheaded woman appeared in his dream, pulling on his
arm to hurry. Why she wanted him to hurry, he could not
see nor comprehend. Nothing looked ominous around them,
yet she jerked him along. Her blouse was open enough that
he could study her firm cleavage and the light freckled skin.
Why was she towing him so? The reason for her obvious
panic escaped him.

He woke up in a cold sweat and sat up on his bedroll. A
thousand stars pricked the sky overhead and a coyote yipped
in the distance. He rubbed his sleep-gritty eyes, then sat
cross-legged and rolled a cigarette for company.

What did the dream about her mean? Damned if he could
figure it. Striking the lucifer, he cupped the flame against
the cool night wind and dragged on the cigarette. He let the
smoke fill his lungs in a deep inhale. Glendora Brown, you
damn sure are bugging me, awake or asleep. He let the
smoke out of his lips slowly, and held the glowing butt in
his fingers. He'd have to learn more about her.

4

"What the hell is going on down the street?" a deputy shouted in the outer office.

"Sounds like a damn Chinese New Year," the other lawman said.

Hailey Ketchem grinned to himself listening to the pair. Whatever was making the deputies scurry around the office in front of the jail was distracting the sound of a harness and a team in the alley behind the jail. He stood on the bench and tried to see the activity.

"That you, Ma?" he hissed.

"Shut up and get back," she said under her breath. "We got a charge to blow the damn wall up."

Hailey jumped off the bunk, grabbed his brother, and they both huddled at the bars.

"Hope it ain't like the last time," Bret fretted. "I never heard myself fart for six weeks, she used so damn much dynamite."

A tremendous explosion in the distance caused Hailey to frown. More diversion, he hoped. Then the whole wall of the rear of the jail exploded into a blinding blast of stinging dirt, dust, and falling boards.

"Get up!" he said, and jerked Bret to his feet. "Come on. See the hole."

Coughing and half blinded, they staggered into the alley.

"Here, take these horses," she directed them. "There's guns in the saddlebags. Ride for Nebraska. You can hide out at the shack."

"What you going to do, Ma?" Bret asked, hanging over from the saddle.

"I'll be up there. Don't get your asses in any jams you can't get out of before I get there."

"Hey, sorry about Arlie," Hailey added.

"Get out of here," she shouted, and they left the alley in a full gallop.

Hailey wondered how she would escape the wrath of the town lawmen, but no doubt they were busy as hell with the fire and explosion that had been set off down the street as a diversion. He whipped the fresh horse and rode like hell for the north. Damn, he hated that hideout in the breaks. No comforts, no pussy in thirty miles, listen to Bret's bitching about it all, and wait for her to come and chew on their butts for Arlie getting killed. Maybe she had the title settled on that farm. It was a better place than that shack in the canyon.

For the moment he had to make sure the horse he rode didn't step into a prairie dog hole, while somehow in this pitch-black night getting free of Dodge's law. He looked back once and saw the ball of flames on the west side of town. It felt good to be free of that damn cow town. It hadn't been anything but grief for them anyway. Good-bye, Dodge—good-bye, Arlie too.

At dawn they rested the spent horses on a small stream. He left Bret and climbed up the high-cut bank to search the country to the south. There was nothing in sight, but they'd ridden their damn horses too hard and the animals wouldn't last much longer. He and Bret needed fresh mounts, and he couldn't see a sign of anything except the simmering heat waves that rose off the brown grass.

He dropped down, half sliding, and joined Bret.

"Gawdamn horses are gone," his brother said. "They ain't worth a whippoorwill pee."

"Get them up that bank. Gone or not, we've got to keep moving."

"They're going to die." Bret shook his head in disbelief and went off leading them into the red stream without taking off his boots. He waded the knee-deep water and sloshed out the other side.

Hailey shook his head in disbelief at Bret, and pulled off both of his boots. Then he started to wade across. Bret was already driving the jaded mounts up the bank to the top. A sharp stick jabbed him in the sole, and he winced as he watched his brother's efforts.

On the far side he sat down and fought his boots back on his wet feet.

"Hard to do, ain't it?" Bret called down to him.

"Yeah," Hailey grunted, using all his strength to get the left boot on.

"Why I never bothered," Bret added, and then spat tobacco.

Hailey didn't looked up. His stupid brother didn't take his boots off crossing a stream because they were too hard to pull on. That was the dumbest reason he could imagine. He rose to his feet and finished stomping the boots on. They felt squashy, but what the hell. He set out up the bank, took the reins to his horse, and began walking northward. Maybe they'd find some fresh mounts later.

He cast a glance back south again—nothing. As he trudged along, the weary, wind-broken horse barely matched his steps. Head hung low, the bay gelding continued coughing as if he had a bearded barley head caught in his throat.

"Why we still leading them?" Bret asked.

"Beats us hauling our saddles ourselves."

"Never thought of that."

Lots of things his older brother never thought of.

"That law from Dodge going to catch us?"

"If they save their horses, hell, they won't be here for two days."

"We got that long?"

"Maybe longer. We ran these ponies all night."

"How far are we from Dodge?"

"Maybe forty miles."

"Forty miles?"

"Gawdamnit, I said it once. You even listening?"

"My ears are still ringing from that dynamite she used on the jail."

"Yeah, well, keep walking. We're bound to find something."

After midday with his belly close to his backbone, Hailey lay belly-down on the edge of a sun-cured corn patch. The bleached leaves rustled as he watched a woman hanging out clothes. Her dugout was beyond her in the hillside, and several tall cottonwoods shaded her large yard. There were some willows along the small stream.

"She alone?" Bret asked, sneaking up beside him.

"She's got a damn dog. He's been sniffing, but can't find us."

"She got any stock?"

"I seen a mare, got a colt."

"Anything else?"

"A mule maybe."

"Jesus, a mule," Bret whispered, and dropped his face down towards the ash-black dirt under him.

"What's wrong now?"

"You'll make me ride him."

"Get up. I don't see no man about and I aim to shoot that black dog first thing."

Hailey rose to his feet in a rush, realizing how tired he was. He drew the Colt his mother had put in his saddlebags. It was loaded with fresh charges. He saw the black dog whirl and start for him with menace in its eyes. The Colt belched smoke and death; the dog yipped in pain and stopped ten feet away. Blood spurted from the bullet hole in its skull, and it began to yelp in pain and circled around like a merry-go-round.

"Get her!" Hailey shouted to his brother as the pale-faced woman screamed with all her might and clutched a pair of wet men's overalls.

The dog at last drove its muzzle in the ground, and Hailey felt satisfied that it would die despite its continued loud moaning. He turned his attention to Bret, who held the woman by the waist. Her high-pitched screaming hurt his sore, ringing ears.

Hailey strode over to her, reached out, slapped her on the face, and she stopped screaming.

"Good," he said. "Where is your man?"

"He'll get you for this." She began to squirm under Bret's arms.

"Answer me, woman." He glanced around to be certain his shooting of the dog had not drawn anyone. No one was in sight.

"What we going to do with her?" Bret acted put out because he was the one having to hold her.

Hailey considered her. A thin woman with stringy black hair, she held little appeal to him. A long face, too big a nose, and thin colorless lips—even her dark eyes were ugly.

"Take her up to that dugout and tie her up. Look around. We need some food and supplies. I'll catch the mare and that mule." He tossed his head toward the sorrel, who had lifted her head in the excitement and was acting watchful while chewing on a mouthful of dry grass.

"You won't get away with this—" the woman protested.

"Yeah, come on, ma'am," Bret grunted as he physically jerked her along.

Hailey turned his attention to their remounts. The mare proved easy to capture and despite her potbelly—no doubt in foal—he liked her. He led her over to where they'd left their spent horses beyond the corn patch, and transferred his saddle. The curious mule could not stand to be out of sight of the mare, and quickly joined them.

Hailey roped him, and then felt better seeing some saddle scars on the mule's wethers. The animal acted walleyed when he cinched Bret's saddle on him, but Hailey ignored his actions, pausing every now and then to listen to the wind that rustled the cottonwoods and the noisy crows that chattered circling above the corn crop.

At last the animals were ready. He led them around to the dugout and hitched them securely to a rear wagon wheel parked before the front door. Where was her old man? Strange, he couldn't see any other planted ground. Maybe over the rise above the dugout they had more. He stuck his head inside, and saw the moonlike butt of his older brother pounding her half on and half off the bed. Bret's pants were down around his boot tops, and he had her skinny legs spread wide and was going for it all with deep grunts.

Hailey ignored them and went to lift the lid on a kettle on the wood range. He used a wooden spoon to dip out and taste the beans. Not bad—it needed some salt. Bret was up to huffing louder by this time. Hailey took a bowl down and filled it with the lukewarm beans. He found a salt cellar on the table and settled into, between bites, watching his brother stuff her full.

Beans needed some salt pork in them, he decided, taking a spoonful, chewing on them slowly, and appreciating Bret's attempts to shove himself clear through her.

She began to moan. It wasn't the cry of a woman in protest. The sounds of her pleasure drew a smile to Hailey's lips. Old Bret was getting to her—the ugly old wench lived out here with some donkey for a husband and never had herself a real screwing. Brother Bret was bringing the devil out in her. He watched her skinny legs close around his brother's back, and she began to hunch her ass towards him. Sunlight coming in the open doorway shone on the long curly black hair on her snow-white shins as she crossed her ankles behind Bret.

Then Bret's back straightened and he raised up with hard effort. By then Hailey was standing beside him and had his pants undone. He moved his brother aside and took his place, sorting her legs aside and jabbing his turgid shaft into her contracting slot.

He looked down at her glazed-over eyes and began to pump her. Her mouth hung open and she huffed for breath, saliva slobbering out of both sides of her mouth. Then she raised her chin up, threw her head back, and screamed like a wounded animal. Wave after wave of contraction grasped his swollen root. He tried with great effort to come, but couldn't. She fainted in a pile. Her legs went limp and he came out of her, still hard, slick, and cramped in pain. He stood over her and silently cursed her. Then he wiped himself dry on her dress skirt and drew up his pants, still erect and hurting. *The bitch!*

Busy feeding his face, Bret grinned. Maybe at his brother's discomfort, maybe at the beans he'd found on the stove top. Hailey went to the doorway, stuck his head out in the bright sun, and squinted to look around. The mare and mule were there. No sign of her man.

"Wonder where he went," he said over his shoulder. Food had no more appeal. Anger and the hard-on in his pants made him ready to ride. He looked back. The ugly woman sat up on the edge of the bed. She was trying to clear the long straight hair from her face. She looked groggy and shaken. His erection began to dissolve the longer he looked at her ugliness.

"Come on, lets ride," he said to his brother. The sooner he didn't have to look at that ugly slut, the better he would be.

"Damn, I ain't through eating."

"Bring it on then," he said, and went to unhitch the mare.

Bret came outside wiping his face on his kerchief and cussing about Hailey always going off in a damn rush. Bret checked the cinch on the mule with little patience. Then he stepped in the stirrup, the mule began to circle on him, and on the second try he made the seat.

"You sure he's broke to ride?"

Hailey never answered his brother. The mule broke into a halfhearted buck, then made a wild dash for the north, and he had to whip the mare to take after them, Bret shouting whoa at the mule and it heeing-hawing its fool head off. All Hailey could see was the whisk-broom tail pumping the mule's gray ass as they went over the next rise ahead of him. Hellfire, first a sorry damn woman faints away on him, then the damn mule runs off with Bret. What else was going to happen to them?

He looked back over his shoulder to be sure the posse from Dodge wasn't on their heels. Nothing out there but the row of cottonwoods along the creek where she'd home-steaded and the heat-simmering brown grassland beyond. Hailey booted the mare faster. Bret and his racing mule were out of sight.

5

Slocum sat on a folding canvas camp stool in the predawn coolness. Estancho was busy making sourdough biscuits, cutting them out on the tailgate with a whiskey jigger by lantern light. A soft morning breeze swept Slocum's unshaven face; he watched the man work.

"What gets you up so early, Señor?"

"A feeling, I guess." Slocum used the first two fingers of his right hand to rub the bristled corners of his mouth.

"What kind of a feeling? If I didn't have to feed these cowboys, my feeling would be to sleep forever."

"Be nice to sleep that long. I get to thinking maybe them Abbott brothers have got a lead on me again."

"How would they do that?"

"Maybe asking folks like that bartender at Doan's Store on the Red River if he saw me go by with an outfit."

"Them two brothers don't ever give up, do they?" Estancho raised up and appraised his work. The white balls of sourdough were neatly patterned in the deep, greased metal pan.

"Like I told you once before, they get paid well to ride my backtrail."

Estancho nodded. "I recall when they came for you in San Antonio that time. That big fat one, Lyle, waving his pistol around and telling everyone in the cantina he would shoot them.''

"Lucky he didn't shoot them.''

"Did you cut their cinches after you left out the back door?''

Slocum shook his head. Maria Mendoza did that for him.

"Man, the fat one, Lyle, he fell off the big Appaloosa horse like *whish*!'' Estancho's words were broken by his laughter, and he continued with effort. "One minute he was waving that big pistol, and the next one he was on his ass in the street and we all had to go inside the cantina to laugh. It was so funny.''

"You think you can handle things until Sam Cantrel gets here Monday?''

"But he owes you your money for this drive.''

"Hell, he'll be lucky to have any britches left after this deal with the price of cattle this low, let alone any money to pay me. Besides, I know where he lives down there. Tell him I'm sorry for leaving and more sorry about how the market turned down on him.''

"Eat some breakfast before you ride out, amigo.'' Estancho put the lid on with a clank; he hauled the oven over and swung it into the bed of ashes. With a shovel, he heaped red-hot coals on the top and at last straightened. He mopped his brow on his sleeve and came back to the tailgate on the chuck wagon.

"I'll stay for your breakfast,'' Slocum agreed.

He planned to take two horses from the remuda as part of his pay. That would be enough for the time being, and someday he would drop by and collect the outstanding balance from Sam.

Slocum and the horse wrangler roped the blue roan and a horse he called Dick from the herd. The stout yellow bay gelding had a habit of running his yard-long pecker out like a stud, which was why the cowboys all called him Dick. The roan was an equally powerful animal, and the two would make him a good string in case he had to flee hard.

For the present, Slocum had no ideas on direction except not back south over the cattle trail—he'd taken a chance bringing two herds up in one summer anyway. It was a wonder they hadn't been waiting for him along the way.

He thanked Bucky, the wrangler, and led the two horses back to load his gear. He intended to borrow some staples from the wagon for his trip. With the pads and sawbuck loaded on the roan, he used two smaller panniers for his foodstuff. Estancho helped him load them with rice, beans, flour, and a few cans of peaches and tomatoes. Then the man ran over to check on his biscuits. In the peachy-colored dawn, Slocum read the nod of approval after Estancho's inspection. The biscuits obviously had not scorched. Lastly Slocum tied down the bedroll on top of the two packs, and was ready to leave out. Estancho was ringing the triangle to come and get it.

The bitter smell of the cooking fires rose in Slocum's nose. He filled his tin plate with steaming biscuits, ladled on the thick flour gravy, took a couple of slabs of fried beef, and went off to enjoy his last meal with the outfit.

He looked up from his meal when a rider came in. Estancho was going around filling coffee cups. Joe Dale slipped off his horse at a respectable distance from camp and came wading over in his bat-wing boots.

"How was Dodge?" Slocum asked, busy with his food.

"Had a helluva thing happen last night. The warehouse for Yates Mercantile blew up. I mean, they must have had tons of blasting powder in it. Then, while everyone was fighting that fire, somebody broke those bank robbers—the Ketchem gang—out of jail."

"The Ketchem gang?"

"Yeah. Blew up the jail, plumb took out the back wall. Killed some horse-stealing breed was in there."

"Ketchems get away?"

"Yeah. They must have had someone with horses waiting to help them."

"Who done all that?"

"They guess another gang member must have done it."

"Sounds exciting. You have a good time?" Slocum asked, cutting off a bite of steak.

Joe Dale shrugged and shook his head. "Wasn't all I thought it would be."

Slocum nodded that he understood. Strange how a man could want to do something so bad for two months—the whole trip up there from Fort Worth—like raise hell in a cow town, and when it was over you felt you still hadn't done what you wanted. Get drunk, mount a wild whore, gamble—do all of it and wake up sober, plumb disappointed, and say, "What did I miss doing that was going to be so great?"

"You fixing to ride out?" Joe Dale asked, taking up a plate.

"In a little while. Estancho's going to ramrod the herd until the boss arrives Monday."

"I'd kind of like that job this winter." The younger man raised up from the kettles, standing straddle-legged and holding his half-filled plate.

"I'll put in the word with the man," Slocum promised.

A small smile swept over the cowboy's face. *"Gracia, amigo."* Then he finished fixing his breakfast.

"You know we can't pay you back what we borrowed?" Joe Dale warned him.

"Leave it with Sam. I'll collect it off him next time I'm back in south Texas."

"Done." Joe Dale nodded and seated himself cross-legged on the ground to begin eating.

The other herders rode in full of questions for Joe Dale. Were the girls pretty? What did they charge? How much was a bath? A new shirt and a shave? The things that the cowboys always asked the experienced ones who'd just returned from town.

Slocum soon told them his plans, shook their hands, and then went by the chuck wagon and clapped Estancho on the shoulder.

"I'm off. Tell Sam that Joe Dale wants to ramrod the outfit this winter up here. He can do it. And tell them Abbotts if you see them I rode east to Philadelphia."

"I would if it would help you. More than likely I'll give them a salute with my Greener and tell them ride their asses away from here. Them two bastards know what I think of them."

"Vaya con Dios, hombre."

"Same to you, *mi amigo.*"

Slocum rode to the west, circled wide of Dodge, seeing on his route several other herds that had not been sold, and then crossed back east headed for the road to Ogallala. He rode with a loose rein, letting the bay take a long trot without much encouragement, and the roan under the light pack trailed easy beside his right stirrup.

At midday, he rode through a shallow creek crossing and noted the narrow hoofprints of mules and iron rims on the sandy banks down into and out of the muddy water. The woman and the boy had crossed there earlier in the day. Obviously she had not stayed for long near Dodge. He rose in the stirrups and seeing nothing to the next horizon in the heat waves, set out on his northward ride.

The sun was far in the west when he spotted the outline of the wagon's bows ahead on the blood-red plains. He drew his horses down to a walk. No harm in stopping to visit if she would talk to him. Besides, she probably didn't know about the Ketchem gang being on the loose out here either. Though he hardly considered them the toughest gang he'd ever met, they were still on the run from the law. The lady and her boy needed to be warned.

"Ma'am," he said, removing his hat in the twilight when he rode up to her campfire.

She eyed him suspiciously, and made no offer for him to dismount. The boy piled out of the wagon and moved defensively to her side to back her.

"Say, it's a big country out here. You have the fire." He

motioned toward it. "And I've got some coffee in my packs we could share."

"Not interested in any coffee," she said, tight-lipped.

"I'm not an outlaw or horse thief and I'm headed north. Figured we'd make some company going there."

"Not interested, mister."

"Slocum."

"I know your name."

"Good enough. There's still some renegades left out here in western Kansas. You and that boy could use an extra gun in case you stumbled on them."

"I thought—"

"Well, the army didn't get all of them. Did you happen to notice their tracks where you scrambled up that last creek bank?" He half turned to look at his backtrail under the low light on the plains. Not even an antelope stirred in the vastness of twilight.

"What about it?"

"You see those two moccasin tracks in the soft mud back there?"

"No." She turned to the boy, who shook his head.

"Then they made them between the time you crossed it and I crossed it." He nodded his head as if in deep thought on the matter.

"Get down, Mr. Slocum. We'll try some of your coffee." She frowned at the boy to dismiss his silent protest.

"Yes, ma'am." He dropped heavily from the saddle and hid the smile on his lips. Those impressions in the sand, why, they'd sure looked like moccasin tracks to him.

6

"I'm hungry enough to eat a whole damn buffalo," Bret said, jerking on his mule's reins while he circled around. The mule kept moving unless Bret dismounted.

"There's some of them left up in the Smoky River country," Hailey said, looking over their backtrail. Nothing back there. They hadn't seen a single soul all day aside from a few loping jackrabbits. He regretted not taking more food from the woman's place. The damn jerky, crackers, and cheese in their saddlebags were something to subsist on, not to eat regularly.

"We better kill one of them before we get to that cabin— damn you, mule, stop." Bret sawed on the reins, but the animal continued going round and round.

Hailey shook his head in disapproval. The damn mule was a complete aggravation unless they were on the move. The place Ma called a cabin in the breaks was nothing but a rough shack that wouldn't make a good wild animal den. The roof leaked—hell, snow even blew in the cracks. Ma's new place was better than that, but folks might find them there. Bret's merry-go-round mule was getting on Hailey's nerves too. He booted the mare out so Bret could ride. Damn thing. They crossed over another ridge.

"What's that?" Hailey squinted to make out the distant figures.

"Injuns," Bret pointed. "Damn Injuns. See them travois?"

"What the hell they doing out here in Kansas?"

"Hunting buffalo, don't you guess?"

"I'd guess anything. Just so them damn Earps ain't on our butts." Hailey looked back again over his shoulder.

"You don't see them, do you?"

"I ain't seen nothing since we run them horses in the ground."

"And we screwed that woman."

"You did that."

"Wasn't my fault she fainted on you." Bret acted amused, holding his bit-gagging mule down to a jog.

"Never mind. You see a war party anywhere out there with them?"

"How come a war party?"

"That's their women and children with the horses and travois, stupid. The men are in a hunting or a war party."

Hailey felt the skin crawl on the back of his neck. He hadn't lived to be thirty-four by exposing himself to bloodthirsty Indians—once more Bret could be kind of dumb about the risk of exposure. Only Hailey's quick actions had saved their hides in some other episodes. Like the time he'd saved the three of them from the whiskey traders. Those black hearts aimed to get them drunk and rob them. Had some young breed girl dancing naked around that campfire. Why, Bret and Arlie were panting like a couple of he dogs after a bitch in heat, guzzling that rotgut and thinking it was all free. Those two buzzards—McKenzie and Wallop were their names—were pouring that firewater out of those crock jugs into the boys' cups, that black man of theirs beating on that damn drum all the while.

What was her name? They called her Morning Star. He could recall the orange and red flashes of the fire splashing over her sleek red skin. She'd rubbed some kind of oil all over her body that made her glisten. Her hands molded her breasts and ran down her hips. Then she beckoned them to come and dance.

Hell, Arlie was up in a minute, staggering around waving his tin cup and talking about laying her. It was only an inkling, but about then Hailey recognized the whiskey runners' plan. There were six mules loaded with prime furs the Ketchems had stolen from two trappers up on the North Platte coming down to Fort Laramie. They'd snuck up and killed them at night, taking the mules and goods. Made the murders look like Injuns did it. Afraid the animals might be recognized, they'd slipped around the fort and taken them east. They'd gotten back on the main road again when they'd met the whiskey dealers, and Hailey now realized those two had one purpose—get the furs.

Before his brothers were too far gone, he slipped off to go piss. With that drum beating away and both Arlie and Bret whooping it up, he stood out in the darkness and made a plan. He'd catch those two traders off guard and shoot them. What he'd do with that black and that girl, he wasn't certain. Might have to kill them too.

His .44 cap-and-ball was loaded. He'd do it with that. Carefully he moved around so he would enter the camp at the traders' backs. They were seated on the ground and clapping their hands to accompany the three dancers. The black man was occupied with the drum. Hailey whipped out his .44 at less than six feet away and in two smoky blasts, shot both traders in the head.

"Gone crazy!" the black man screamed, jumped to his feet, and raced off howling into the night.

"Why you do that?" Bret asked, looking dismayed.

"They aimed to get us drunk and steal our furs. Arlie, get her."

The boy caught the wide-eyed brown-skinned girl by the arm. Too shocked to run away, she looked blank-faced at the two crumpled men on the ground.

"What about that black?" Bret asked.

"He'll get lost and die out there." Hailey shrugged off his importance. What was the word of some ex-slave going to mean against them anyway? "We need to drag these two away from the road and scalp them, so they think Injuns done it."

"What about her?" Arlie asked with a foolish grin.

"Do whatever you want with her." Hailey smiled at him knowingly.

"Hot damn. Come on, girl, I've got something for you." Arlie pulled her toward their gear piled on the ground.

"Here," Hailey said to his older brother. "Get a pack mule so we can take their bodies out of here."

"And he has all the fun," Bret said in disgust.

"He can't wear her out. There will be plenty of her ass left when we get back."

"This is going to be lots of work."

Already bent over and busy emptying their purses and taking their knives and weapons, Hailey looked up and scowled at him. "Get going. It will be dawn in a few hours and we need to be gone from here."

Now, while he studied the band of Indians on the horizon, Hailey wished they still had the liquor they took from those traders. Nothing like whiskey to lubricate Indian men and women. The whiskey makers' cargo had brought more than the furs in the end. He glanced back across the prairie—nothing.

Ahead he could make out a few men with the women. They were dressed in ragged, filthy clothing, had trade muskets, and walked at the head of the procession. The wide-eyed children grew silent at the outlaws' approach, and hid bashfully behind the heavily burdened thin horses. Even the few dogs under packs were silent. The women who carried papooses and backpacks avoided looking at the outlaws.

"What kind are they?" Bret asked under his breath.

"Maybe Cheyennes. Let me handle this." He raised his right hand and advanced toward the stalled train, leaving behind his brother circling his mule.

"Ho!" he shouted in his deepest voice.

A tall man with gray-streaked hair and one eagle feather fluttering in his thick braids came out. He wore a dirty gray blanket and carried a single-shot rifle across his chest.

"My name is Hailey Ketchem. I am friend of Indians."

The man stopped fifteen feet short of him. Then he nodded to indicate he'd heard him.

"Are there any buffalo left to kill out here?" Hailey asked.

The Indian made a sweep to the west with his gun arm holding the barrel up to indicate where the buffalo were.

"Do you look for them?"

The man nodded.

"We want a buffalo to eat. We would share it with our red brothers."

The man nodded.

"Good. We will be partners. You can have the hide. We will share the meat." Hailey felt the man must understand, and turned in the saddle to look for Bret. The mule still circled, and Bret drove the impatient animal up to join him.

"He speak English?" Bret asked.

Hailey shrugged. "Don't matter, we're all going hunting us some buffalo."

"Speak good English," the Indian said. "We go look for buffalo. Fine. But you don't fuck my wives or play mean tricks on my children."

"Fair enough," Hailey said, a little taken aback by the man's clear-spoken words.

Bret agreed with a nod on his circling mule. In desperation, he at last dismounted and the mule began to bray raucously. His hee-haws drew smiles from the Indians. Finally Bret slugged the mule in the face to make him stop, and only hurt his hand. Wringing and waving his fist about in anguish only amused the Indians more. The mule kept on braying.

"Quit that, Bret," Hailey said with impatience. Why did

he have to go and make such an ass out of himself when they were trying to impress these savages?

"How far away are those buffalo?" Hailey asked the chief.

"Maybe two days, maybe a week."

Gawdamn! That old fart didn't know a dang thing more about them than *they* did. Why, they could ride around all over hell looking for them.

"Gray Wolf my name."

"Hailey. That's Bret with the barking mule."

"Want him to quit?"

"Hell, yes."

Gray Wolf stepped before the animal, held his hands over the mule's nostrils, said something to the animal, and silenced him. The animal dropped his head and his brown eyes studied the chief. Then, as if in a spell, he lowered his face and the chief ran his palm down the entire length from his ears to his nose twice.

"Well, I'll be damned," Bret muttered. "How did you do that? That damn mule ain't been that settled since we stole—I mean, bought him."

Gray Wolf put the blanket back on his shoulder despite the heat and stepped back. "We must go on or we will not make water by night."

"Go ahead, we're with you." Hailey motioned for him to go on. They would be coming along.

"What have you got figured about them?" Bret asked as they held back and let the train go ahead.

"They need something to eat, it looks like to me."

"You see that bright-eyed girl in the yellow buckskin looking at us?" Bret hefted his crotch like it was bothering him and stared after the procession.

"Make damn sure she ain't one of the chief's wives," Hailey said under his breath above the hiss of the travois poles and the slaps of women beating the burdened horses with quirts to make them move on again. The squaws' guttural words scolding the horses and dogs made them go—but at a slow pace.

In late afternoon they reached a river with strong current for a plains stream. The muddy brown water swirled around an ancient dead cottonwood sprawled out into the course. Quickly several woman disrobed and with a large net began to spread out across the knee-deep water.

"What they trying to do?" Bret asked.

"Catch fish, I guess," Hailey said, watching closely the prettier ones with flat bellies and pear-shaped breasts. Some had floppy tits; others had watermelon-sized ones and bellies to match in late pregnancy. As if unaware anyone watched them, they chattered and laughed. One fell down and quickly bobbed up, drawing much mirth from the rest.

Upstream several nearly naked boys on sweat-stained horses free of their loads began to make them prance and dance as they beat the water with branches. They whooped and made war cries. The water became frothed with the horses's actions, and the squaws nodded in approval, holding their nets down with sticks so no fish could escape under their fence.

When the boys drew closer, the women on the far bank began to stalk around in a circle with the net. There were more laughs and some more dunkings, but the trap became closed and the riders sat their jaded animals. Others came to the bank, and soon the crude net was hauled up on the grass. Several sparkling fish flopped in the mesh, and Hailey moved closer to see their efforts. He was impressed at the catch.

Turtles, crayfish, carp, suckers, and catfish were imprisoned in the net as the women spread it out on the buffalo grass.

One woman gathered the crayfish. Expertly she reached in, grasped them, and deposited her catch without a pincer finding her fingers. Some of the older children plucked up a crustacean, then quickly tore off the tail, discarded the head portion, peeled the tail open, and ate it raw as if ravished.

Two younger squaws with shapely bare butts were bent over, untangling the various fish and tossing them to the cleaners sitting cross-legged on the ground. These women whacked the floppers on the head with a rock, gutted them, and laid them aside. The work went fast. A floppy-breasted woman without front teeth busied herself gathering the small turtles into a sack. Some of the children helped her, making faces at the turtles that when held up tried frantically to escape and swim in midair.

"Plenty to eat tonight," Hailey said to the chief.

The man nodded his approval. "Yes, but fish don't make a man's dick stiff like buffalo meat."

Hailey glanced at the fiery sunset flooding the western sky and the far horizon. Would they ever find a buffalo to eat? Maybe. He hoped so.

7

In the twilight, Slocum busied himself unsaddling Dick and the roan. Glendora had already ground the coffee beans in a hand grinder, and he looked forward to a cup as he piled his things on the grass and then hobbled his horses. He could have used a bath and shave back at Dodge, but that opportunity had come and gone.

She rose up from stirring her fire. "Guess you have business up north?"

"Supposed to be lots of interest in she-stock and starting ranches from here to Canada. I thought I might find enough people needing mother cows and I could bring up a herd for them next spring."

"You deal in cattle?" She indicated a canvas folding chair, and took one herself close by.

"I brought two herds of steers up to Dodge this year for other men. Got here a little late with the second one and the market's off bad. May have to winter them up here somewhere."

The boy joined them, looking fresh-washed and shiny in the last light of the day. He sat cross-legged on the ground, acting interested in something out in the growing twilight.

"My husband is working a homestead in Nebraska," she said.

"And his name is—"

"Cy Brown."

"I heard of a Cy Brown once—" Slocum cut off his words and shook his head. "Couldn't be the same man." An empty feeling filled his gut at the knowledge. The Cy Brown he knew had been hung by vigilantes the past spring for raping and killing a woman. Slocum recalled his cold trip across Nebraska in March. He was so anxious to get back to Texas and make the first drive of the season, he took the Holiday stage line from Fort Laramie to Omaha, then passage on a river boat down to Arkansas, and then a fast horse to meet Sam Cantrel in San Antonio by the first of April. On the stage to Omaha, they were delayed for some repairs, and everyone during the stopover was talking about the lynching of Cy Brown, who'd strangled some whore with his bare hands.

"Might be him," the boy injected. "Paw's been awful busy up here getting the ranch ready for us."

"Jeremy, I am certain Mr. Slocum in his travels has met several men with similar names. Brown and Cy are both common names."

The boy shrugged.

"Our place is south of Ogallala about twenty miles," she said.

"He been up there long?"

"Yes, over a year and a half. I think that coffee smells ready," she said, and rose to get cups off the wagon tailgate.

Slocum sniffed the air. The coffee smelled ready to him too. What if her man had been the Cy Brown they'd hung? She'd learn it all in due time. He didn't need to bring grief to her life. Glendora had broad shoulders like most Western women, and would make the best of things. Let her discover the truth for herself, and if she needed support he would be there. Any woman who set out by herself from Texas with a boy in his teens, four mules, and a string of colts to tag along had enough gumption to make it anywhere, even on a Nebraska homestead.

The coffee tasted rich, and later her steaming red beans proved flavorful. The skillet corn bread reminded Slocum of his raising in Georgia.

"Do you have a place of your own?" she asked, shattering the silence of the open plains.

"No, ma'am. I guess I'm kind of rootless. Lots of country out here to see."

"You've been to that place they call Yellowstone?" the boy asked.

"Yes. Amazing place. They have more hot springs and mud pots bubbling up than a man could ever see in a lifetime."

"I heard if you breathed them, they'd kill you."

"Never killed me. There's whole valleys where steam rises winter or summer and hisses off in the air."

"What causes it?"

"I guess lots of heat under the ground. Some of them roar too."

"I'd like to go there and see it."

"Some big waterfalls too."

"How far is it from, say, Ogallala?" the boy asked.

"Maybe thirty days."

"How's that?"

"The Indians say Yellowstone is twenty sleeps from Fort Laramie. That means in travel it is twenty days. I figure in ten you can get to Laramie."

The boy dropped his head. "I'd hoped it was closer."

"In time, Jeremy, you can go there if you still want to," his mother assured him.

"Still want to go there?" the boy said with a wary shake of his head. "I always will want to go there and see that steam and stuff."

"You know you have your whole life ahead of you."

"I guess, Ma."

She turned to Slocum. "How expensive are cows?"

"I guess you could get some good she-stuff up here for twenty dollars. Be three to five years old and the solid kind of cows that have several calves left in their hide.'' He felt embarrassed by his blunt reply, a kind of raw way to talk to a lady, and looked off at the first star to twinkle in the sky.

"I couldn't buy many at that price."

"What you need to do then is buy the limpers. Every herd has some footsore cattle won't hardly drive that they usually have to leave or shoot them. They're mostly too thin to eat for beef. A good ramrod will sell them for a dollar a head. See, that way the boss gets something out of them and he knows he's going to lose them before they reach their destination."

"What will they need? I mean what kind of care?"

"Oh, water and graze. They'll heal up and get fat on this buffalo grass. Be easy to catch for a while and when they get well, they'll know where your place is too."

"You make it sound interesting. We could afford some of them. Now when will the herds come up here?"

"Probably be some more this fall with the cattle market so weak and the only demand for she-stock up north of here. They ought to wag their tails up here right along till late fall."

"What if they're steers? These limpers, as you call them."

"Heck, a fat steer later will sell for as much as two cows. Make oxen out of them while they're sore-footed and you can handle them. Why, a broke team of oxen would bring enough to buy six cows."

"Sounds exciting, doesn't it, Jeremy? Maybe your father and you can do that."

"Yes, ma'am. Them ox as hard to break as these mules were?" he asked Slocum.

Slocum looked across at the boy. "You and your mother break those four mules?"

"We sure did, or we'd've got up here a month ago."

"I am sure Mr. Slocum doesn't want to hear about our mule breaking."

"I sure would like to hear, Jeremy." Slocum scooted forward on the chair to listen.

"I'll do dishes," she said, sounding a little put out, and rose to gather the plates and silverware from them. "Another cup of coffee?"

"Yes, I'd have some," Slocum said.

"Well, we bought those mules from a Kraut—"

"A German man," his mother corrected him. "His name's Mr. Renshauser." She returned with the coffeepot and began to refill their cups.

"Anyway, Renshauser said those mules were broke and he had plowed lots of land with them. We led them home and harnessed them up. They acted awfully anxious, and Mother worried we didn't have them hooked up as teams like he had done them, so we switched them. Only, then they were worse, so we changed them back."

She shook her head in disapproval, and busied herself kneeling down at the tub of soapy water washing dishes and kettles.

"See, we had this old wagon," Jeremy said. "Not the one we have now. It's a lot better rig than the first one."

"And something spooked them," she coaxed the boy, and made a displeased look at Slocum.

"All hell broke loose, to be exact."

"Jeremy!"

"It really did. The mules stampeded. Ma caught a hold of the wagon going by, and I rushed after Booger, my horse, to try and head them. Those mules could sure run."

"And you hung on to the wagon?" Slocum asked her in disbelief.

"Hung on and pulled myself up going off across north Texas like a whirlwind. That wagon flew from one bump to another, and when I managed to get in the box, I worked my way to the front, intending to get the lines we had tied up to the brake. First one wagon bow slapped me on the head, then the opposite one did, and I fell down in the bed

I don't know how many times." She looked to the dark sky for help.

"While she was doing that, I was trying to catch her on Booger, but those mules could run like a skinned rabbit. The north branch was less than half a mile ahead, and I knew they'd wreck it all and kill themselves going off that bank. I started hollering, 'Jump off, Ma!' "

"I couldn't hear him over the thunder of those mules and wagon and all. But I finally got the reins and tried to stand up behind the wagon seat."

"A back wheel came off. The dust got so bad I couldn't see a thing," Jeremy said.

"The other one went next," she said, busy drying the plates with a sack towel.

"That really made a dust storm, but me and Booger were getting closer."

"I managed to swing the teams around and head them for the ranch on the very brink of that cut-bank." She shook her head and looked impressed at the towel in her hand. "It was a flat miracle."

"I caught up then," Jeremy said, "and she was getting the hair out of her face with her fists full of those lines. She said, 'Get back, Jeremy. These damn mules can run away, they can run back home for a lesson.' And she went to laying the leather to them, making them race back to our place with no wheels in the back."

"That was their first lesson," she said with finality, and rose to her feet. "Be early in the morning, son. Better find them quilts of yours."

"Yes, ma'am. Night, Mr. Slocum."

"Slocum's fine. My friends call me that."

"I will then. Good night."

"Good night, son."

Slocum rolled himself a cigarette from the makings in his vest pocket. He offered her one, but she declined, and he struck a lucifer alive with his thumbnail in a burst of light to torch the end. He drew deep and planned to enjoy the full length of it before turning in.

"I don't believe there was a moccasin track in that sand," she began in a very low voice. "But I'll not argue with your company. You're a gentleman. What is it you know about Cy Brown that I don't?"

8

Busy breaking camp to move on, the squaws hustled around loading horses and dogs in the half-light. Everything moved smoothly. Hailey noticed for the first time the sound of the small bells they wore on their leggings. Some were braided into their horses' manes. It had been part of the camp noise before, mixed in with the guttural talking and the yips of dogs stepped on or kicked for being out of place. The ringing made a musical background to all the activity. A fog of fine dust began to boil up under the women's soles as they hurried about their duties, busy as always taking down and packing the animals. They seemed to know where everything went, and everything had a place.

Still full of the fish feast from the night before, Hailey ignored the offers of the women to eat some leftovers. His mouth tasted as muddy as the nearby stream from the previous evening's meal. Those boiled crayfish needed some pepper sauce. He'd eaten a bushel of them in Louisiana, and hot spices really helped them. The catfish baked in mud were the next best, but the Indians liked the bony suckers and carp better. The turtle soup had a visceral flavor, and he'd only sampled it.

"She ain't his wife or daughter," Bret said under his breath while they saddled their horses.

"You're certain?"

"I'm certain."

"How the hell can you be sure she ain't lying. She speak any English?"

"No, she makes sign language."

"Gawdamnit, Bret, you're as bad at that as I am. She might mean you could fuck her mother or her horse."

"We never talked about that."

"Keep your damn pecker in your pants. I don't want to have to butcher a damn buffalo by ourselves if we get one. We can get the good cuts out of one and this army of squaws will do all the work, unless you piss him off messing with his women. We're going to need that meat if we're going to hole up in that shack."

"How long? How long we holing up there?"

"Till things cool off some."

"The damn weather's going to do that and soon."

"Forget that bitch and ride your mule."

"I think that gawdamn chief cast a spell on him. See how good he acts today?" Bret finished saddling him, then scowled at the patient-acting mule.

"Maybe he did. Maybe he did. They got ways to do that." Hailey shook his head. He didn't know what Indians did with animals, but he'd heard of them casting spells on creatures. It sure wouldn't have hurt that braying bastard to have two spells cast on him. Hailey mounted the mare and reined her up. Bret did the same with the mule.

"I believe he *did* do something to him," Hailey said, and booted the mare over to where Gray Wolf stood with the half-dozen other bucks.

"Bret and I will look south for sign of buffalo, and circle back this afternoon. Will you go straight west?"

Gray Wolf nodded, and used his arm like a railroad semaphore to indicate the direction.

"Is there water there?" Hailey tossed his head in that direction.

"A small lake, if it is not dry."

"We will look for sign and if we don't find any, we'll locate you this afternoon. You think they are out here? Buffalo?" He looked hard at the dark-faced man with high cheekbones and the deep lines in his facial skin.

"Yes, some are still here."

"Good, we all need the meat," Hailey said, seeing Bret making sign language with the girl who stood back alongside the train. He ought to kick his brother's ass.

"Find a fat buffalo, we trade him a wife," Gray Wolf said smugly.

"In that case, he'll look twice as hard," Hailey said in disgust, then raised his voice. "Come on, Bret, they want to go."

The sun rose and began to warm the rolling vast grassland. Yellow green hoppers swarmed in small clouds before them. They flew head-high with a man on horseback, and then lighted on the dry grass and sage until the vegetation was covered with a mass of squirming hoppers.

The Indians soon disappeared over the rise, and Hailey and Bret headed in a long circle to the south. Hailey squinted against the harsh sun, hoping and then even imagining in the glare that some distant dot was an animal. Nothing, not even a stupid antelope. Prairie dogs in great patches of tunneled land whistled at them, then ducked from sight. He swung around them.

"We find a damn buffalo and I get that squaw, we can take her with us to the cabin," Bret said, sounding like he had been considering the matter for some time.

"How long you reckon Ma will let her stay?"

"I'll tell her I married her."

"Ha, she ain't about to claim no damn breed as her grandchild. Why, she'll run her ass off quicker than you can click your tongue."

"Maybe I won't let her."

Hailey shook his head. Fat chance Bret would have going against that woman. She'd have her damn way about that squaw or Hell would freeze plumb solid.

"You'd have to leave the country," Hailey said.

"She ain't my damn boss. I'm—about thirty-three years old and I can do what I want."

"Long as she agrees you can."

At midday they found a water course and a line of cottonwoods. They rode along the ten-foot-high bank until they reached a crossing, and dropped off to water their horses in the shallow sluggish stream.

"Look," Hailey said, trying to dismount, hanging his boot in the stirrup, and having a hard time extracting it. Good thing the mare was gentle or he'd have been dragged to death. He at last drew his boot free and scowled at his own clumsiness.

"What?" Bret asked from the other side, watering his horse.

"Tracks."

"What are they?"

"Cloven hooves, look like buffalos to me."

"They been here?" Bret stood on his toes to see over Hailey's saddle.

"Yeah, they've been here. Been a couple days ago, but we better split up and check this creek."

"How far should we ride?"

"You ride a couple miles downstream, I'll ride a couple up. Don't spook them if you can help it."

"How many are there?"

"Six to ten, I'd say."

"Whew, be a whole herd. He might give us both wives."

"Quit worrying about pussy and go find the damn buffalo."

Bret shrugged and remounted his mule. "You sure get bossy."

"Someone has to do the thinking for this outfit." Hailey fought down the rest of his anger. Bret had his damn nerve accusing him of being bossy. Someone had to take the lead for this outfit, and all his brother could think about was screwing some danged old squaw. If Ma Ketchem showed up and found him rutting some red sow, there would be hell to pay in camp. He didn't want to hear all that yakking.

Bret rode off in a huff and he let him go, remounting and riding the opposite way. It would be nice to find some fat buffalo to eat. The lush grass and the water would insure the animals they found would be in good flesh—if the buffalo hadn't gotten a notion to leave it and gone off out on the plains. It didn't take long in the heat with no water to gaunt them up—out there a week and their meat would be too tough to even boil.

He smelled whiffs of smoke on the wind, and looked back over his shoulder. Bret was nowhere in sight, already gone. Who had a fire? Maybe buffalo hunters? Hailey checked the Colt on his hip. Most of them were riffraff, wanted men seeking an existence out of killing the last scattered bunches and selling the hides. Didn't even jerk the meat, left it to rot. He'd not seen any buzzards or prairie wolves, so maybe they had not found the herd yet. Wouldn't be long, though, if they were looking for them. This late summer drought would keep the animals from venturing away from the streams.

Hailey could see wagons ahead in the trees and frowned. They weren't ordinary wagons with canvas tops. Some were painted orange and some green. What the hell were they? Gypsies. What were they doing way out there? Only thing Gypsies knew how to do was trade horses and steal. Sure couldn't get much through larceny in these parts, and the horse trading would be slim pickings too.

He could hear a squeeze organ and people clapping. Damn, they were having a party and dancing in this heat. A mouth harp broke into the polka music, and cautiously he booted the mare in close enough to see what was going on.

"Hello," a sharp-nosed dark-complected woman said to him.

"What the hell are you Gypsies doing out here?" he asked.

"We like to wander. This your land?" she asked over the music and noise.

"Hell, no," he said, intently watching the flash of the girls' shapely calves when they kicked. Round and round, they danced with arms locked in a line. Heel, toe, heel, toe—he shook his head, must be fifty or more of them.

"Get down and have a drink," the woman offered.

"I believe I will," he said, still intrigued by the beauty of the dancers as they circled around in their line.

"You want some wine?" she asked, holding a dusky brown bottle up to pour him some.

Quickly he found his tin cup and held it out for her to drain the red wine into.

"What are you people doing here?" he asked. "There are hostile Indians all over this prairie."

"They don't want us."

"I ain't so sure."

"What are you?"

"A hunter. You seen any buffalo?"

She shook her head and looked at him hard with her coal-black eyes. He guessed her to be in her thirties. Her breasts looked interesting under the colorful red material.

"How far to the next town?" she asked.

"Dodge is about two days that way."

"What is there?"

"Saloons and whore—I mean some hotels and cattle pens."

"What is west?"

"More hostile Injuns."

"You hunt by yourself?"

He shook his head. The dance over, the girls were sweeping the hair back from their faces, laughing freely, and dipping water out of a barrel to sip with long-handled gourds. Good thing he found this camp—Bret might have gone crazy; all these attractive women in one place. He needed to guide his brother around them.

"Sit down, you look hot," the woman said.

"No," he said absently, turning over in his mind the oddity of this many Gypsies so far from civilization.

"You have any meat for sale?" she asked.

"I might, if I find the herd."

She stepped in close and placed her long fingers on his arm. Her deep olive skin covered a web of black veins. A gold ring flashed in the overhead sunshine and she squeezed him.

"We could pay for it."

He glanced down again at the over-familiar hand, and then into her face. In his pants he felt a stirring of his manhood. He tested it with a push from inside, and like a muscular serpent it responded. Without a word, he nodded that he understood what she meant.

Then he drew back his shoulders. "If we get any killed, I'll come back and look for you. Your name's?"

"Agatha."

"Agatha," he repeated, then mounted the mare before the Gypsy discovered what her hand had done to stir him. Damn, because of her, he faced an uncomfortable afternoon with a stiff dick and nothing to poke it into. Hailey rode away from the camp knowing her eyes were boring holes in his back. At a distance, he reached down and adjusted his crotch—but the stone ache only grew worse.

9

The cigarette smoke drifting up smarted his right eye. Slocum used his little finger to flick off the ash, then turned his full attention to her. She scooted the full skirt under her and sat down on the adjoining camp stool. The obvious intent on her face was to learn everything he knew about Cy Brown.

"Early last March I came out of Fort Laramie by stage," he said. "Headed for Omaha. We stopped at place called Lacey for repairs to the coach. I heard talk from the locals saying the vigilantes just lynched a man by the name of Cy Brown in Ogallala." He paused before he took the last drag off the roll-your-own. "He could have been anyone."

She didn't reply. He drew on the cigarette, watched her, and inhaled; she never looked up at him. He ground the butt out and stripped it between his fingers. Still she did not look up.

"I got the last letter from him in February," she finally said in a small voice. "I kept expecting him to come back to Texas for us. First, I thought he was busy putting out a crop—then no letter. Well, maybe it got lost, lots of mail does that. But he'd be coming for the boy and me. Then when spring passed, I decided we better come see what was wrong and I bought the mules—well, you heard the rest of the story.''

"It might not have been him.''

"What did this Cy Brown do to get himself hung?'' She raised her face like a condemned person facing a judge's sentence and looked him hard in the eye.

"Raped and strangled a woman.''

Her thick lashes squeezed shut, and she curled her hands into fists in her lap. The upper portion of her body shook with the fury of her revulsion.

"Could your man do that?'' he asked softly.

"I don't know, Mr. Slocum. I really don't know.''

"Was he violent?''

"Sometimes angry—I would never have thought of him as a man who would strangle . . . a woman. No, that does not make sense about the man I married fifteen years ago.''

"He was in the war?''

"Yes, he saw several battles east of the Mississippi. He wasn't no stay-home Texas guard boy.''

"The war changed him?''

"We all changed during the war. Damn renegades ran through the countryside robbing and looting unchecked. Women and children were nearly defenseless and without food.''

"Been a while since then. Why did he come up here?''

"Wanted a new start for us. He was restless in Texas. Land we had was poor, hot, and dry. He thought—'' She drew a deep breath. "He said we could have a good farm up here where the soil was rich and virgin.''

"He must have a claim. I mean a homestead. You and the boy can reclaim it.''

"I could pray the next hundred miles it wasn't him too—couldn't I?''

"Yes, you could, and I'd swear to God I hope it wasn't him.''

"Mr. Slocum, thanks.''

"Folks call me Slocum.''

"Folks call me Dora."

"Good night, Dora."

"Night, Slocum."

For a long while, he sat on his bedroll and let the night wind cool him from the day's heat. There was no way to know if her man had been the same one they'd hung. She had broad shoulders; Dora Brown measured up to be a survivor in his book. She'd lived through the war, broken wild mules with a boy in his teens, driven them across Texas, the Indian Territory, and most of Kansas. She would survive the truth about her man if he was the one they'd hung. Slocum inhaled the sharp smell of dried grass and sagebrush. Maybe he'd help them a while if it was so. There was a lot of woman in that dress to look at; maybe if she needed the assistance, he'd stay around. In a few days they'd know the truth. The Platte River ferry crossing wasn't more than a three-day drive north of them.

Dawn came on the arms of prelight that ignited the prairie in a soft glow. Slocum unlimbered himself from his blankets. The boy went off whistling to get the mules, who were hobbled, and their brays soon broke the rest of the predawn silence.

"Coffee is about finished," she said over her shoulder when Slocum walked up. She poured coals on the Dutch oven with a shovel, then straightened up. "Kind of you to share that coffee with us."

"Eating your food, ain't I?"

"That's nothing. Since we haven't seen any Indians, I figured you were anxious to ride on—see about those cattle, cows, whatever. We'd only be holding you back and all."

"There are still bands of hostile Indians out here," he said, holding out his cup for her to pour him some coffee.

"Guess they'd want more than four mules and some thin yearling colts."

"They ain't choosy. They don't leave witnesses either."

"I figure Jeremy and I can handle any blanket—any Indian comes around."

"Fine, I'll ride on to Ogallala. Look for you there in a few days."

"Ain't that I don't appreciate your services and all." She swept the stubborn wave of hair back from her face. "But how would it look, me riding into town and looking for my husband and another man along that isn't even a relative or even a friend of his?"

"It would look safe to me."

"Well, I have to think about how it would look to Cy too."

"No more needs to be said. I'll haul my freight."

"Have breakfast first." She looked at him sincerely with her wide green eyes.

"I'll sure do that, ma'am."

"Dora."

"Yes."

He watched the shape and motion of her willowy hips when she busied herself swinging out the Dutch oven from the ashes. Then she removed the lid and nodded in approval. Jeremy had the four mules tied to the wagon when she called for him to wash his hands. Breakfast was ready.

Slocum shook hands with Jeremy after the meal, and thanked Dora. She tried to give him the rest of the coffee beans, but he made her keep them. One last look at her shapely form and a knot began to gather in the pit of his stomach. It was a mixture of upset over parting with such a fine-looking woman, and concern over how it would turn out in the end for her and the boy.

He saddled Dick, packed his things on the roan, and set out for Ogallala. He waved to them as they harnessed their teams, and left in a short lope across the prairie, scattering yellow grasshoppers in his wake like popcorn. Maybe when he reached town he could learn about the dead Cy Brown and find out where he lived.

It was past dark when he crossed the Platte on the ferry and rode the rest of the way into Ogallala. The main street was dark except for the strips of light from some of the noisy establishments. The patches of illumination spread out into the middle of the roadway. Hitch rails were crowded with hip-shot horses, and several tarped-down freight wagons were parked in the thoroughfare and left for the night.

The shrieks of women's screams and laughter, tinny piano tunes, and the music of squeeze boxes blended with the roar of men's voices. Slocum reined around two staggering drunks who came propelled into the street and almost ran into him.

"Welcome to Olie-gah," the close one slurred, and waved a floppy hat at him in passing. In the darkness with the light from the saloons falling out on the hitched animals, Slocum carefully eyed the horses he passed. Texas cow ponies for the most part, none he recognized. It was too dark to see their brands. At the end of two blocks, he went around the corner and dismounted.

It had been early morning since he ate, and his throat felt full of trail dust. He hitched his horses at a nearby empty rack and loosened the cinches enough to let them rest. Then, with his eye on a cafe across the street, out of habit he reset the Colt on his hip and waded across to the far boardwalk.

The place looked half full, and he came inside the open door and took a place at the counter.

"Well, you old son of Texas," the sharp-eyed woman in the blue-checkered dress said with more snap in her voice than an ordinary waitress. "What'll it be? Half a dead steer or a dozen scrambled eggs?"

He used his thumb to loosen the sweat-glued band of his hat and tilt it back on his head. "Ma'am, I couldn't eat that much in a week."

"Good, you aren't a liar like the rest of them." She waved a small tablet at the others busy eating.

"Beef sounds good."

"I've got some fried, with some rice, gravy, and light bread?"

"Coffee on the side," he added, nodding in approval. "You got a basin to wash up?"

"Right out the back door on the table. Make yourself at home and I'll get you some food."

He rose and moved through the narrow room behind the men busy eating and talking. They hardly looked up at his passage. He nodded to the pimple-faced boy doing dishes in the hot kitchen, and saw the sassy woman talking to a big man in an apron who was red-faced from hard work and the kitchen's scalding temperature.

It was cooler in the alley. He poured fresh water in the basin, soaped his hands and then his face, rinsed them, then used an old sacking hung there and dried himself. That felt better.

"You're new in town, ain't you?" she asked when he came out from under the towel. Blocking the doorway, she smoked a cigarette. He could tell it would be a quick one because she already looked ready to toss it away and go back inside.

"Yes, ma'am."

"Name's Tissie. I get off work in an hour."

"Be obliged, but I have horses to tend to."

She flipped the cigarette away, forming a red arch into the darkness of the alleyway.

"Just mentioned it in case you were interested." That said, she went back inside on a turn of her heels.

Slocum smiled after her. He reset his Stetson on his head and followed her inside. After a sharp word at the cook, she disappeared with a flash of her shapely butt into the dining room with two plates of food.

"Women," the cook said, and slapped his forehead with the palm of his hand. "What made her so mad at me?"

The pimply-faced boy shook his head, and Slocum nodded to both of them and went on in. He found his seat, and she delivered him a cup and prepared to pour him coffee.

"You ever hear of a fella around here named Cy Brown?" he asked.

She paused and looked at him hard. "Yes, they hung the son of a bitch last spring. Why, you knew him?"

"He owed me. He have a farm or ranch anything?"

"He had the Blue Belle whorehouse down the street and he gambled a lot. He choked one of the girls to death in a mad drunk rage—wasn't the first time he'd done that either. The others he killed were 'accidents.' Convenient as hell, wasn't it?"

"They try him?"

"A trial here? An angry lynch mob done it and the bastard deserved it. How much he owe you?"

"I don't guess I'll ever see it again. He's the only Cy Brown in the country?"

"Only one I know," she said, straightening from filling his cup. Then she waved the granite pot in front of a grizzly-faced man busy chewing on his food. "There any other Cy Browns around here, Malcolm?"

"Just that one they hung." The man nodded as if considering the matter, then satisfied, went back to feeding his face.

"Guess you've lost your money, mister." She gave him a crooked grin and went off in a dash.

"Guess I did." He wondered what Dora and her son would do when they learned the news. Obviously, her late husband had not been farming land—the lady was in for a real shock at his true profession in this place. The food came and despite the fact that it was tasty, the bites did not go down easy. Slocum's mind was on Dora and the shock she would have at the discovery of the truth.

10

Hailey spotted his brother riding his mule hard across the prairie and waving his hat at him. He glanced back to be certain the Gypsies were far enough back that Bret couldn't see them. What did Bret want anyway? No telling about his idiot brother; Hailey put spurs to his mare and rode out to meet him.

"What is it?"

"Buffalo—" Out of breath, and his mule huffing for his wind too, Bret swallowed hard. "I seen four of them."

"Good. You didn't scare them, did you?"

"No. Damn, they are in a deep-cut creek getting a drinking. Right over this hill. What—we going to do now?"

"Go tell Gray Wolf."

"Damn. Reckon he'll give her to me?" His sweaty face lit up at the prospect.

"Quit worrying about pussy, I told you. We need to go get Gray Wolf and the tribe. We can get us a big bait of jerky and loin out of this deal, and we can live on that for months up at the shack." He wondered how he could slip back and give Agatha some of it. She'd be grateful enough she might give him a little of something else. But enough thinking about that dark-eyed Gypsy. They'd better get busy and find Gray Wolf.

Hailey set the mare northward in a long trot. They should catch up with the band in an hour or two. How would they kill the damn buffalo? The Indians had some old trade rifles, and neither he nor Bret had a good carbine. Maybe ride in close and shoot them in the head with a pistol—he'd heard of folks doing that. Buffalo were hardheaded, but any way to kill them was okay. Maybe the chief would have a better idea.

They caught up with the tribe by midday. Gray Wolf and the other four bucks considered the news, acting a little shocked that Bret had located four of the animals.

Grey Wolf gave a squaw an order, and then nodded to Hailey. "We must have sacred time to pray to our gods. Then we can go and kill all four of them."

Displeased with anything that would slow their return to find the buffalo, Hailey looked at the high sun to check the time of day. He hoped that the Cheyenne realized those woolly buggers weren't tied up back there. Why, they could be out of the country in no time at all.

"First we must talk to spirits," Gray Wolf said adamantly.

"Don't be long at it," Hailey said, acting displeased, and went to where Bret sat his calm mule.

"What're they doing with that sagebrush?" Bret asked, indicating the Indians.

"Got to have some kinda sacred ceremony before they go kill the buffalo."

"Lord, them damn things may be in Montana by then."

"Hush up. We ain't got no choice in the matter." Hailey undid his cinch, and then dropped to the ground and listened to the bells. Seated on his butt, he watched the women rush about to make the fire in the center of the men's circle. Maybe he would learn something about their religion. It sure wasn't Baptist.

That Preacher Guthrey had tried to drown him in the river. Held him under extra long to purge the sins from his heart that the old coot said he saw inside Hailey. Enough to turn a man off from religion altogether. It was a wonder he didn't drown in that fishy-tasting water. And next time he saw the pious bastard, he was in Ollie Lawrey's log barn, sticking his pecker into the oldest Lawrey girl from behind. The preacher was panting about the wonderment of it all while Hailey peeked through a knothole and tried not to sneeze from the musty hay. Wide-eyed, he took in the whole operation with the awe of a boy in his teens. Mary Beth Lawrey was her name. She had buck teeth and freckles and the snow-whitest butt he'd ever seen with her dress thrown up over her back. No wonder Guthrey did it from behind. It would have made even that preacher sick to have to look in her ugly face for that long a time. Why, before it was over, Hailey got so excited watching them do it that he spotted his pants too.

She must have gotten pregnant from doing it with him, because she had a hurried-up wedding later that summer to a man from over in Bald Mountain, Tennessee; Cecil Fossil was his name. The name for the community he lived in must have come from him. He had the highest forehead of any man Hailey had ever seen, and an Adam's apple that bobbed in his throat like a fishing cork with a perch on the line.

Hailey could recall wondering, when he heard later Mary Beth had a baby in the fall, if it looked like old round-faced Guthrey or her long-faced husband. But he never saw her again, nor did he ever see the offspring. A short while after that their ma took them all to Missouri. They appropriated some horse stock, loaded their bedding and her few pots and pans, and took leave of Tennessee under cover of night. Arlie Joe Ray was still a kid, and kept asking when they'd get there. Damn, Hailey got tired of him asking that all the time.

Hailey looked across to where the Indians were singing. "Hey, yo! Hey, yo!" was all he could hear. The song went on and on, like a wailing with a tune that waved like thick grass did in the wind. It would start again and keep going. Nothing like hymns where you sang a few verses and quit when you ran out of them. Here it was same words, different pitch. They were taking deep sniffs of the sagebrush smoke too. The boom of the drum carried, and finally Gray Wolf stood up and faced the east, spread out his arms, and let the blanket fall away. He looked sort of skinny standing there in his loincloth. His ribs showed even that far away, and his arms were like the drawn muscles on a dead horse's leg.

He was talking to his God. Just like Guthrey did at services. Then, from the corner of his eyes, Hailey saw the women had taken the travois poles and packs from the horses, and the horses were in war paint with yellow and red and black symbols painted on them. One bay horse they brought up looked like he was bleeding; the red war paint was over his eye and half his head.

Gray Wolf mounted a short-coupled roan and rode over to Hailey. "We are ready to kill the buffalo."

Hailey rose to his feet and looked around. There was no sign of Bret. Where in hell's name had that idiot gone? He drew up his girth, stalling for time. Soon Bret came from beyond the camp, pulling up his pants and ignoring the stares of the bucks who had joined Gray Wolf.

"What in the hell you been doing?" Hailey asked between his teeth.

"Taking a shit. Why?" Bret fixed his girth and the two mounted up.

"Thought you were doing something else." Then Hailey pushed his mare close to Gray Wolf.

"We have few guns."

"You have pistol. You kill one. Him kill one. Brave Elk kill one with rifle." He motioned to a big-nosed buck on the red-painted bay. "Gray Wolf kill one with spear." The chief hoisted his thick-shafted spear with a razor-sharp shiny metal point wrapped on the end of it.

Hailey considered how close they had to get to the buffalo for a kill with a handgun. Within yards to shoot and stop them. That would be close, closer than he wanted to be to them, but they were committed. No way to back out.

"They were wallowing in the mud like hawgs," Bret said.

"Gnats are bad." Hailey's stomach churned at the thought of being in mad pursuit of one of them, firing away, and the buffalo turning his sharp horns into the mare's belly and slicing open her bowels. That was what could happen—and what about her rider? He drew a short breath and shook his head to drive out the fear. He had to do this, even if he was careful and didn't get too close; he needed to make an effort.

Two hours later they huddled behind a ridge. Bret pointed to the cut over the hill.

"They were down in that creek. It's about ten or twelve feet deep and narrow."

"Which way did they look?" Gray Wolf asked.

"Oh, you mean which way were their heads facing?" He pointed to the east and then the west. "Half and half."

"Some were looking both ways," Hailey added.

"High bank on the other side?" Gray Wolf asked.

"Yes. I don't know how they got down in there," Bret offered.

Gray Wolf sent two men to circle west and two to circle east. Then he pointed to the two brothers. "You must each get one with your pistols."

"We'll try," Hailey said, not certain he had the strength to even draw his Colt out of the holster. The thought of this encounter with a herd of buffalo had drained his strength and made his stomach so queasy he felt ready to vomit.

"He ever mention me getting her?" Bret asked in his ear.

"No, but we better get one buffalo each."

They mounted up and charged from the top of the hill. The Indians were screaming, and ran right up to the brink of the deep gorge. The muddy, wet buffalo had already taken off and were racing through the red water and slop as fast as they could. Hailey leaned over on the mare as it raced hard on top of the bank. He didn't hear the Indians screaming any longer. He drew his six-gun as the mare charged along the edge of the gorge, the prairie footing helping her overtake the lead bison. Mouth open and grunting hard, the buffalo put on a new burst of speed, realizing like a rabbit with an eagle over him that Hailey was on the bank.

He took aim and fired the handgun. It bucked in his hand, and the mare shied a half-pace but kept up her race. The buffalo went on unimpeded. Hailey shot again, and saw a splash of mud from the .44 slug in the animal's muddy neck. Too far back. He raised up, took a wavering aim from the rocking gait of the horse, and shot again. The buffalo's front end crumpled and then in an end-over-end cartwheel, it disappeared in a muddy splash. Damn, he'd gotten it. How lucky! He had his buffalo down, and began to rein in the mare. Then he looked up and saw twenty feet ahead a deep side cut that blocked their path. Its width and depth matched the one beside them. It was way too wide for the mare to ever jump it. He was unable to stop her as she gathered herself to go over it, then flew out into open space.

He shook loose of the stirrups in midair, the Colt still in one hand, the other one outstretched for a handhold that did not exist. He and the mare went down toward the reddish mud and sluggish stream beneath them like floating leaves, falling forever. The roar of protest from his mouth was so loud it hurt his ears.

11

In the dark alley, Slocum rested his back against the wagon box and smoked his second roll-your-own. With the horses long stabled, he waited in the shadows while voices from the kitchen carried to him. Tissie knew more about Cy Brown than she'd told him. There had to be some explanation. He couldn't believe that Glendora Brown had ever married someone like that. The damn war had changed many men, but still, no one usually changed that much.

Maybe there was a picture of the dead man. The newspapers liked to publish those pictures of dead men on boards after hangings and killings. They'd done the same thing in Dodge with that bank robber Ketchem. Slocum would have to see about that in the morning. Dora would be in town by then. Maybe there was a slim chance this Brown wasn't her husband after all. The only thing wrong with that theory— where would her man be?

"Whew," Tissie said, and threw a shawl over her shoulders as she came to stand in the lighted doorway. "Every part of me aches," she said to the others leaving the kitchen.

"Sounds bad," Slocum said in a soft voice when he stepped out of the shadows.

"Oh!" she cried. "Thought you had horses to tend to."

"A man could change his mind."

He saw a sly grin sweep her face. "Yeah, a man sure could."

She stuck her arm in the crook of his and they went off up the alleyway. He glanced back and saw the outline of the cook in the doorway scratching his head. He probably wondered how he'd missed out and someone else had lucked in.

"You never said your name," she declared.

"Slocum."

"That's all?"

"That's enough, ain't it?"

"Yeah," she said, gathering his arm up more into hers. "Least it ain't Jones or Smith." Then she laughed openly with her head tossed back. She put a little swagger in her walk, and on purpose bumped her hip into his. "I kind of figured when I first laid eyes on you that you had some life left in you, Slocum."

"A little."

"Aw, hell. How did Brown ever owe you money?"

"Didn't really." They paused, made sure nothing was coming, then crossed the street. "I met his wife and son on the way up here. She doesn't believe her husband would have done such a thing."

"He was a pervert." Slocum could see her lip curl in the faint light as she led him up the narrow staircase to the second floor of a building. Obviously, Tissie had no use for the man.

"Don't make sense," Slocum said. "He was a farmer and family man back in Texas."

"Maybe this fella said he was Brown and wasn't." She shrugged her shoulders and then opened the door. "Be stuffy in here. This should help." And she crossed the room and threw open two windows.

"His wife got letters from him until last February."

"Hell, I don't know." She moved in close and took a hold of his vest in both hands. On her toes, she poised her mouth for him to kiss in the room's silver darkness. The night wind tossed the lace curtains. He took her in his arms and kissed her.

"Who's the law in this place?" he asked, and drew a deep breath. He looked over the top of her head and out the window into the night.

"Lacy Dutton. He's a stick-in-the-mud." She ran her fingers up and down the seamed edge of his vest.

"Where was he when they hung Brown?"

"Out of town."

"Convenient as hell, wasn't it?"

"Yeah, it was. He'd gone up to Fort Laramie to get a prisoner that afternoon."

"Who was that?"

"Damned if I know, but the man wasn't up there or something. I remember he got back in a big huff about the lynching. It was the next afternoon on the stage and he had no prisoner."

"What else can you tell me?"

"Nothing. I guess all you came up here for was to learn what I know?" she asked.

"For now. Maybe another time. When I have more time."

She nodded her head. "You got lots of things on your mind, huh?"

"I'd like to know more about this Brown mess. This all isn't adding up. Things are too damn neat. The law leaves town, the prisoner is lynched."

"Well, he wasn't a nice person!"

"What do you mean by that?"

"I mean I hated the sumbitch and was glad they hung him." She folded her arms over her chest and stalked over to the window with her back to him.

"All right, Tissie. If you think of anything let me know," he said, and started for the door.

"I will," she said, and walked over to him.

"Things ain't bad here. What happened to your man?" he asked, looking around.

"Left me." She shook her head mildly as if she didn't have an answer for that either.

"What the hell for?"

"Went to Montana, never came back."

"Got killed?"

"No. I figure he didn't find any big riches after all that big talk he made and couldn't come back and face me."

"What's his name?"

"Coyle. Why you asking?"

Slocum shook his head. "He must be a full-sized fool."

"Ah, hell, pride can kill a damn fool man. He ain't alone, there's plenty more like him." She acted as if it all meant nothing, but she couldn't hide her feelings despite the facade she tried to put up for him. "Went off up there to get rich and never did nothing, and he can't stand to ride back here and tell me that's what happened," she said over her shoulder.

"Ain't nothing else you can tell me about Brown?"

"Mean sumbitch. He probably killed two other girls. The doc said they took an overdose of laudanum, but one of the other girls, Sadie, she told me he strangled each of them for hiding money from him. He had a bad temper. He got into it in the saloon in a card game one night. That time it was over two dollars. Took four men to hold him down while the cowboy escaped."

"His wife said the war changed him."

"Maybe. All I know is I hated him. What will you do for her now?"

"Damned if I know. She's come clear up here. Just her and a young boy, maybe twelve."

"Slocum." She came over and playfully swung on his arm. "Hey, he did have a place down on the Platte somewhere. They butchered cattle all the time down there to feed the girls. Word was his men weren't too fussy about the brands."

"Where is this place?"

"You could find out at the land office. By this time, someone maybe squatted on it."

"If he owned it, his wife would be entitled to it."

Tissie agreed with a nod. "Bet it ain't much more than a soddy in a hillside and some pens."

"Be better than nothing."

• "Go see Thomas Farenger in the morning. He runs the land office." She tried to twist him around to face the door.

"You reckon Coyle will ever come back to you?"

She shook her head. "Got too damn much stubborn pride."

"Maybe he needs some sense pounded into him?"

"Don't bother."

Slocum filed the matter away. Right now he needed to learn about this possible farm or ranch. If Brown owned the whorehouse, maybe Dora had money coming from its proceeds.

"You need a place to sleep . . ." She paused with a wry set to her full lips and looked hard at him.

"Thanks, maybe when this is all over. . . ."

She shook her head to dismiss him, then gave him a bright smile. "Good luck with your *business.*"

"I may need it." He touched his hat brim for her, then went out the door and down the stairs. He chided himself for not taking advantage of what she'd offered. Tissie was an attractive enough woman, alone and willing. He took the stairs quickly down to the alley. The cool night breeze swept his face when he reached the ground. He glanced up the stairs, but there was no sign of her. He went on.

He walked slowly back to the livery, and slept until dawn in the loft. At sunup, he washed his face and hands in the horse trough, then took breakfast in the diner. There was no sign of Tissie there. He still had regrets about not taking her up on her offer to stay the night. Outside in the street he looked both ways, then spotted the land office sign, and headed that way on the boardwalk. He wondered if it was open this early, but seeing a man working inside, he entered the office.

"Morning," the agent said cordially.

"Morning, I need a little help."

"What can I do for you?"

"This man Brown they hung last spring. He owned some property round here?"

"You his kin?" The man looked at him suspiciously.

"A friend of his widow."

"Yes, he owned eighty acres across the Platte." The agent turned to his maps, and shuffled through the stack until he found the one he wanted.

"Anyone have a claim on it?" Slocum asked.

The man shook his head. "I don't believe so."

"What about the whorehouse?"

Oh, he owed money on it. The bank had a mortgage and foreclosed on it. They didn't consider the eighty worth filing on, I guess."

"What happened to all of Brown's money?"

The man's face paled. He shook his head. "I have no idea."

"Did someone steal it?'

"I—don't know."

"Guess I better speak to the sheriff about that?" It sounded to Slocum as if there was something wrong about the matter and the man didn't want to talk about it.

"Yes," the man said, sounding relieved. "The sheriff would be the one."

"How do I get to this place on the Platte?"

The agent spread the large map on the counter and smoothed it out. "Here is the Brady Crossing. The property starts a half mile west of there."

"It has some improvements on it?"

The man frowned at him. "I guess you know about it?"

"Some. What should I know? Was it a den for rustlers?"

"Oh, I don't know about that."

"Thanks, you've been a big help."

"I never caught your name."

"Slocum," he said, and went out the door. What would he tell Glendora Brown? Her husband was a whoremaster and a rustler? Things only grew worse. He drew a deep breath and tried to put all the information together. He couldn't.

He headed for the sheriff's office next. The man might have a wanted poster on him, but he wanted to know more about this Brown before Dora arrived.

He entered the office, and a man in his twenties with his dusty boots on the rolltop desk looked up at him. "What kin I do for you?"

"Sheriff in?"

"I'm the head deputy. I can handle it." He took out a jackknife and began to clean his fingernails and eye Slocum at the same time.

"When will he be back?"

"I said I can handle your problem, mister," The deputy swung his feet around and planted them on the floor.

"Good. Who lynched Cy Brown?"

"Who's asking?" The deputy's face began to redden.

"I am. John Slocum."

"I don't figure that's any of your gawdamn business, mister. But vigilantes did it."

"Guess you're holding Brown's assets for probate court, aren't you?"

"What?" The deputy bolted to his feet. "You some gawddamn highfalutin lawyer?"

"Are you holding the estate?"

"Why, hell, no, we ain't. Brown owed my—the bank a sizeable mortgage and they took it. All legal and nice. No, there ain't no damn money left."

"Good day," Slocum said, and started to leave the lawman.

"Hey, who you representing?"

"The family," Slocum said, and hurried out the door and across the street.

12

The pain-filled screams of the mare brought Hailey to an awareness. His right leg was painfully pinned under her right side. Covered with slippery mud, he fought for his Colt. She needed to be put out of her misery. If she continued struggling, she would hurt him even more. She could even break his leg. He drew back the hammer with his thumb, and the gritty metal part fell on a dud. Fighting to free his foot from under her, he rearmed the revolver. This time it roared in his hand, and the mare stiffened in death. A bloody spot mixed with the syrupy mud showed behind her ears. Using his other boot to push off the mud-coated saddle, he finally came free.

Out of breath and shaken, he sat on his butt and flung the sloppy coating off his hand and weapon. His saddle was in the mud and the mare was dead. His only consolation was he was still alive. He flexed his right leg. It was sore, but nothing felt broken. Then, with effort, he glanced up at the high bank.

"You all right?" his pale-faced brother asked, leaning over the edge.

"No, gawdamnit, I've lost my horse. I'm covered in this goo." He struggled to his feet, finding the footing very slick.

At last he stood with his boots apart. "Where's the damn buffalo?"

"We got three of them, I think."

"Good," he said, leaning over to look back up the draw. Seeing nothing, he waded the shin-deep water to the main channel. He arrived in time to see Gray Wolf and two other bucks eating raw liver. They held it high and screamed, waving for him to come join them in their feast. His stomach roiled at the notion, and he shook his head.

How the hell would they ever get the meat out of this mess? Ignoring the Indians calling to him, he went back and undid his cinch. He looked around for his brother.

"Throw me down a rope," he shouted, and Bret's face appeared.

"I'll get it."

Hailey waited, filled with impatience. What could happen next? He looked up. The rope wasn't long enough. He bent over and fumbled at the mud-coated lariat on his saddle. When it was free at last, he waded over and tied it on the end of Bret's rope.

"Tie it to the mule and pull the saddle free," he shouted after hitching his end to the horn. He stepped back, unsteady on the slick footing. The rope drew taunt and dirt fell from the bank above where the lariat cut in and tightened. At last the saddle began to ease out from under the mare's corpse. Hailey moved around and lifted her limp head to remove the bridle. His leg hurt like fire.

"That's good!" he shouted. When the saddle was clear of the horse, he looked in disgust at the mud-caked rig. He'd never get the damn thing clean again. He flung the brown slime off his hand and tied the head stall on the saddle.

"Now take it up," he shouted.

The saddle disappeared over the lip of the ravine. And he began to slog around in search of a way out. No way to get out appeared; only steep sides faced him. In reluctance, he decided to join the Indians.

"Where you going?" Bret asked from above.

"To see what the damn Indians know." He sloshed through the slop, which almost sucked his sodden boots off in some places. The water grew deeper; then he managed to find a shallow place. Several topless squaws were busy in the mud and water skinning the buffalo as though they were on dry ground. The animal blood mixed in with the brownish water in red streaks.

"Fat!" Gray Wolf shouted, holding a mud-coated piece of viscera in his face.

"Much food," Hailey agreed, thinking about the gritty sand that would get behind his molars after every bite.

"You tough hunter." Gray Wolf clapped him on the shoulder. "Give you war horse to replace mare. Wonder why good hunter ride mare."

"She was powerful," he said, regretting her demise.

"Have wings."

"Not enough," he said, more to himself than the chief. The copper smell of butchering filled his nose and flowed into his mouth. The women, muddy to their elbows, worked to separate the hide from the meat.

One young squaw with her long breasts dipped in the brown syrup and mud streaks across her face held up a bloody knife, taking a short rest from her skinning and grinning at him. The zeal of her butchering had obviously unleashed some form of excitement and charity towards him. Maybe later he could find out how much she appreciated him.

They worked for hours, at last hauling the buffalo up by quarters on to the grass. The women took pails of the creek water and wads of grass to wash away the mud, but he thought the process hopeless. Men lounged about and smoked clay pipes. The first haunches of buffalo were cooked on smoky fires.

The mud dried on his canvas pants and they stiffened. He had scraped and worked to rid his boots of most of it. They were stuck upside down to dry on sticks stuck in the ground. He tried to remove the grit from his pistol, but the only thing he had to clean it with was mud-soaked and the process was slow. Seated cross-legged on the ground, he noticed his brother had gone off somewhere. Obviously to pant over that squaw he had his eye on. They needed to take a big haunch of the buffalo meat and head for the Platte.

He glanced up. Some squaw was bringing him a chunk of cooked roast on a stick. The burned black edges surrounded the rich brown-coated meat.

"You eat first," she announced in good enough English that it shocked him.

He drew out his knife and looked for a place to wipe off the dirty blade. She glanced down at the side of her leather skirt, and he leaned forward and used it, sharing a private look with her as the screaming children gathered around them. He cut free a chunk, sharing a grin with the short squaw. The meat was still pink, but tasted rich and flavorful in his mouth. He offered her some off his knife, and she took it.

He began to cut chunks off and feed the children, who stuffed handfuls in their mouths. They were obviously starving. Soon the meat was gone and the squaw ran back for more. The children had grease running off their chins, and between bites chattered in Cheyenne to each other. The feast had begun.

He looked around for Bret. No sign of him. Gray Wolf came by with a boy leading a red paint. Both of the horse's ears were cropped off and he had one watch eye. The animal was broad-chested, and looked sound and powerful enough despite Hailey's personal dislike of the breed.

"Make great war horse," the chief said. "Warrior should ride a horse with plenty balls." He hefted his own loincloth with his hand to demonstrate his words.

Hailey nodded in gratitude. "Fine horse. I will ride him with pride."

The woman came back with more rare meat on a stick. Then she took a place on the ground beside him. Gray Wolf nodded in approval and went back to his party. Everyone seemed engrossed in eating. Hailey ran his tongue around his mouth trying to loosen the telltale grit from behind his teeth.

"More!" She shoved the meat on the stick at him.

Yes, he would have more. "What is your name?"

Her words came out in the guttural language, and he caught only the "Kay" part.

"Call you Kay," he said, and pointed at her.

She nodded, then bent over and stuck the stick with the meat on it in the ground, close enough that he could cut off a chuck when he wanted. He whittled her off some, and she nodded, taking a place by him. The paint stallion, staked close by, gave a studlike whistle. He glanced around to see the animal had his multicolored dick run out and was hunched down and jacking himself off.

Slocum turned back and tried to pay attention to eating more buffalo.

"Him like you?" she asked softly, nodding her head toward the stud horse.

He nodded uncomfortably and busied himself eating. In a short while he felt about to bust from overconsumption. He sprawled out on his back and studied the pale blue sky. Buzzards had begun to circle. Some dove down into the ravine, while others lazily floated above him waiting with patience for their share. Camp dogs charged the braver ones that landed too close.

Kay rose and went for something. He didn't really care. Soon she returned with blankets and a robe on her arm.

"We go over there," she said, standing above him.

"Fine," he said, standing up in his still-damp mud-caked clothing.

They went around some low-growing bushes, and she spread out the robe on the ground. He stood in his stocking feet and watched her. With a flurry she unfurled the blanket. Then she took off her blouse and dropped the leather-fringed skirt. Seeing her naked standing before him, he felt a growing need in his pants. He stripped off his vest and shirt and dropped his pants.

She stepped in close and began to stroke his manhood with her small hand. His stomach rolled over and an urgency began to build in him. He motioned toward the ground, and she nodded. In an instant, she was on her back. He glanced around, saw no one, and out of breath prepared to plunge his throbbing erection into her. Then he knew, even as he hurried to stuff himself inside of her, that his gun was going off. Barely inside her slick entrance, his cannon fired and he closed his eyes to reality. He had come. Gawdamnit!

13

Slocum saddled his horse at the livery. With no sign of the woman and boy yet, he decided to ride south and try to intercept them. They had a place in the brakes, he knew that much. Not where a man wanting to farm would have chosen, but it might make a horse ranch for them. He still couldn't get over his deep concern for the pair. Never mind her good looks; he short-loped the gelding toward the river south of town.

He used the ferry to cross the river. The operator had not seen the woman and boy, so he resumed his riding south up through the bluffs that bordered the river on the south bank. These were the brakes, and they stretched for miles along the south shore of the Platte, forming a labyrinth of canyons that separated the rolling prairie from the river. It was a broken country where men could hide from the law and themselves.

On top, he rose in the stirrups, expecting to see the oval of the covered top on her wagon. Nothing in sight. He short-loped the horse on. Where were they? They should have at least made it to there by this time.

Late afternoon, he crossed a shallow river in a deep cut and rode up the far bank. He recognized an outline of the familiar wagon out on the prairie, and headed for it. He spotted her shielding her face from the sun with her hands to look at him.

"Slocum, is something wrong?" she asked, coming to meet him.

"No," he said, and dismounted from his hard-breathing horse. "I was concerned when you weren't on the road."

"Jeremy and I had to shoe one of the team." She held her hands on her waist. Obviously the work had strained her back. "So we put off moving until tomorrow. You learn anything up there?"

"You can claim a ranch. It's about eighty acres in the brakes. Not hardly farmland. The business he operated was taken over by the bank, and no one seems to know about any money he had left."

"Business?" she asked with a frown.

"A whorehouse," he said quickly.

"Oh, my God. It's worse than I thought."

"The Brown they hung ran the place. He also butchered cattle at his ranch and brought the meat to town to feed— well, his employees. Some say it might have been stolen beef."

"A whorehouse? Rustling?" She used both hands to push the windswept stray hair back from her face. She avoided looking at him.

"Dora, I didn't come back here to tell you lies. That was what the man was doing."

"What'll I tell Jeremy?"

"The truth."

"I guess I will have to. You mentioned money?"

"A man operating such a business had money. No one wants to talk about it."

"I don't care about that filthy money."

"Wait. You and that boy have to survive up here for the next year. If he had money, you need it."

"How will we get it?"

"Go to the sheriff and demand it." He noticed the boy's

horse missing, and searched around for him. "Where is he at?"

"Took the rifle and went hunting."

"Fine, just wondered. You get those shoes on all right."

"Yes." She braced her hands on her waist and straightened again. "Say, I've got some of your coffee. How about a cup?"

"I'll take it."

"How hard is this place to find? This place in the brakes."

"A good day's drive west and north. I have the directions."

"Guess we start for there in the morning."

He nodded. "Yes, but I don't expect a lot. May be pretty rough."

"I won't expect a palace, Slocum," she said, pouring him coffee in a tin cup.

"Good. I figure it is just a dugout and some pens maybe."

"I've lived in worse."

He agreed, and blew on the hot coffee. It was too warm to dare taste, though the rich smell drew the saliva in his mouth. Maybe they could get set up before the north winds blew snow.

"Do you reckon he'll find anything? Jeremy?"

"Oh, maybe an antelope. Buffalo are getting scarce and the deer are almost all gone."

"He's a good shot and killed deer before in Texas."

"I may wander out and see if I can find him. In case he needs some help." He looked up, and she had her back to him. But the quaking of her shoulders told him she was crying.

"You going to be all right?" he asked softly.

"I imagine so. No, I'll be fine. I guess I hoped all the way it wasn't my man they hung for doing some dreadful thing. Now I must accept the truth. I can't go on lying any longer to myself or Jeremy."

"Be the best."

"What did they say he did?"

"Strangled one of the whores in a mad fit over her holding out money on him."

"War's hell, Slocum. I sent a good man off to war. He came back changed, but I never knew how much."

"It changed us all, Dora."

He rose, and she came to him and wept on his vest. He tossed the cup aside and held her.

"Why are you here?" she asked, wiping the tears from her lids and skin.

He offered her his kerchief. She thanked him and used it. Then she buried her face in his chest again. He held her tight enough to reassure her he was there to help.

"It worked out this way," he said.

"But I ran you off yesterday when I knew you were only trying to help me."

"I don't run far."

"Thank God." She straightened up and used the kerchief to dab her eyes some more. "I'll wash it out for you." She meant the cloth.

"I think that horse has his breath back. It's mid-afternoon. I'll go look for Jeremy."

"Then I'll be back in your debt again." Her eyes glistened with tears.

"Be a big bill too," he said with a laugh, and cinched up the horse. He swung in the saddle.

"You two don't find any game, we can eat beans. I'm cooking some of them."

"Be plenty good enough for me. See you." He rode away with a wave.

The boy's tracks led to the southeast, and he followed them easily. He crossed the next rise and not seeing any sign, looked back toward the wagon. She should be all right until he returned. There was nothing out there to bother her. With the horse in a long trot, he searched across the dazzling afternoon heat waves for the boy, easily following the tracks of his pony.

He dropped off into a brushy depression where a line of gnarled cottonwoods lined a shallow river. Riding his horse and looking back over his shoulder hard, he saw the pale-faced Jeremy coming toward him.

"Hey," he shouted to get the youth's attention.

"Slocum, that you?"

"Yes. What's wrong?"

"I almost rode in on a big camp of Injuns back there. They were having a war dance."

"How many?" Slocum asked, surprised there were any around.

"I don't know, but they were dancing and having them a war party."

"Maybe celebrating?"

"Maybe."

"See any game?"

"Seen some tracks I figured were a day old or so that a few buffalos made. I was riding up them, but they led me right to the Injuns."

"Injuns must have found them first. Probably celebrating a kill."

Jeremy glanced back, and then turned to face Slocum with a wry expression on his smooth face. "I'd sure like to have killed one of them. Then me and Ma would have enough meat for winter. I don't figure we'll find him around when we get to Ogallala. We won't, will we?"

Slocum shook his head. "There's his ranch, but it may be very plain."

"She know about it?"

"Yes, she does."

"How did she take it?"

"Hard. We better make tracks. If there are Indians out here, we best get back to her."

"Yes, sir."

Slocum looked back to the southwest, and wondered

about the Indians. They might have been starving and happened on those buffalo. A successful hunt would trigger a big celebration—the boy probably only saw them having a victory dance. He hoped so, and set the horse into a trot. It would be better when they were back with Dora. He and the boy would both rest easier.

"Are there any other buffalos left out here?" Jeremy asked.

"A few, I guess. Might be more west of the main road. We get things set up, I'll go with you and look for one."

"I'd sure like to kill me one."

"We'll try to find one for you to shoot."

"Thanks, Slocum. I'm glad you came along. Ma will realize one day he ain't ever coming back."

Slocum twisted in the saddle and looked hard at the youth.

"He ain't coming back," Jeremy said. "I knew that a long time ago, but I couldn't tell her. She's hard to tell things at times. Gets her mind set on something."

"I think she's ready to talk to you now," Slocum said, and they rode on.

"Indians?" she asked, wide-eyed at Jeremy's story. Her eyes searched Slocum for an answer.

He shook his head to dismiss her concern. "A band out searching for food is all. They didn't offer to chase him or anything. I think they killed some buffalo and were having a celebration."

"But what if he had rode into their camp? Oh, Jeremy, you better not—"

"He did the right thing, Dora," Slocum said to defend the boy. "You said we'd have beans."

"Yes," she said, and carried her skirts as she walked to the campfire and the suspended kettle over the smoky fire.

Jeremy shared a private glance of gratitude with him, and they both turned to watch her stir the beans. He hoped he'd saved the youth some unnecessary motherly hobbling. The boy knew it too.

"You two coming? Why do I feel this is some kind of conspiracy against me?"

"Ma, we wouldn't do that."

"Hmmm. Get a plate and I'll fill it. Shame those Indians wouldn't share that buffalo with you two *men*."

After supper, Jeremy rounded up the colts, and Slocum helped him hobble them to save making the young horses easy prey for an Indian raid. By the time they finished, the sun had died in a fiery ball in the west and some prairie wolves had begun to howl.

Slocum smoked a small cigar. Jeremy had turned in his blankets. The long day's adventure no doubt would let him easily find sleep.

"Can we reach the ranch tomorrow?" she asked, breaking into his thoughts.

"Or get close."

"Good. I owe you an apology."

He shook his head to dismiss her concern as the soft light of twilight settled across the rolling land.

"Yes, two days ago I deliberately asked you to leave. Now I am embarrassed and also grateful you returned."

He drew on the stub and then inhaled the smoke. Slowly he exhaled. "No problem."

"You are a drover. What else are you?"

"A man who rides on."

"Oh, I never heard it said like that. A man who rides on. Strange, but why?"

"Let's say I have to keep moving."

He snuffed out the cigar on the iron rim of the wagon wheel, watching carefully for a spark. There was no rhyme, no reason to his life at all. Come the next day or the one after that, he'd leave before the bounty men on his heels found him. His lifelong sentence meant no lengthy stays, like all winter in a dugout with a voluptuous woman like Glendora Brown. He studied the first stars dotting the sky. There was no way he could stay until spring. They'd come for him before then.

"Good night, Slocum," she said in a soft voice, and gathering her skirts, went to her bedroll.

Good night, Mrs. Brown. He drew in a heady breath of the sweet prairie smell as the day's heat went down and a gentle night wind rose. It took away some of the bitterness that from time to time poisoned his days.

14

The squaw Kay disappeared from the blankets sometime in the night. Obviously, his poor performance in bed had disappointed her and she'd left him. Hailey didn't care. She stank like campfire smoke and horse. He moved about the camp in the cool predawn searching for Bret. They needed to move on. Part of the buffalo meat was theirs. Hell, they didn't need to wait around for it to become jerky. He was ready to ride and if Bret wanted to rut his squaw, he could stay with the damn Indians for all Hailey cared. For his part, Hailey wanted to be the hell out of this damn dog-sniffing camp.

"I'm ready to ride," he said, squatting on his boot heels beside where his brother lay under the robes.

"Huh?" Bret blinked his sleepy eyes.

"Get your ass up. We're riding out of here."

Bret rose up on his elbows. "What's the damn rush?"

"I've had enough Injun."

His brother glanced around, looking for her. Then he threw back the covers and stood up to pull on his britches. Mumbling to himself, he reached for his shirt and gave Hailey a disgusted scowl, putting his arm in a sleeve.

"I'm taking her along."

"Suit yourself. Ma will run her off."

"Then I'll leave."

"Yeah, like you have enough money. That's why we tried to rob that bank in Dodge. Did you forget? We're flat broke."

"These Injuns don't have money. They get by."

"Yeah, sure is wonderful living. When the first snow blows, sleeping on the ground ain't going to be so gawdamn nice."

"I ain't leaving her."

"Then get her ready to go." Hailey could hear his stallion whistling. The sound made him anxious and angry. The stupid stud and his brother made a pair for him to put up with. Not to mention the squaw he had to bring along with them. Ma would hate her—he didn't look forward to her response to Bret's concubine. She'd have a fit.

In an hour, Bret had his horse and his woman's two horses loaded. They shook hands with Gray Wolf, ready to leave.

"Good hunter. You could stay," the chief offered to Hailey.

He felt uncomfortable. The squaw Kay kept peeking around some of the others to stare at him. He nodded good-bye to the chief as he saw that Bret had his woman mounted.

"Maybe we will meet again." Hailey gave the chief a salute, then mounted his stallion. The paint danced around, and he checked him with a frown. It was a powerful animal, and his muscular form and spirit presented a change for Hailey to ride. He reined him around and waved at the rest of the band. The last face he saw was the hard, unmoved face of the squaw Kay. Displeased with her persistent glaring at him, he set the paint into a trot.

They rode all day. Hailey pushed them hard. By late afternoon he realized they would never reach the hideout before dark and they had to spend another night on the ground in the open.

"We better make camp," he finally told his brother.

"There might be water at that line of cottonwoods."

Hailey agreed with him, and turned in the saddle to check their backtrail, then glanced over at the squaw. Riding her bay pony and leading the pack animal, she smiled at him. He turned away. She probably stank like that damn Kay. The notion made him sick to his stomach.

When they camped by the stream, she made a fire with some dry wood she gathered and buffalo chips. The two men sat on the ground, upwind from her fire, and talked.

"We need to find us some rich fella to rob," Bret said, scowling in disgust and jabbing the fire with a stick to flame up the wood. "What are we going to do for money?"

Hailey shook his head. Arlie was dead. Only two of them were left. They needed a gang to pull off anything but a petty robbery. They used to rob stragglers on the Oregon Trail. But that was too dangerous now that the towns were getting settled. Maybe Ma would have a good plan.

"You ain't got any ideas what to do?" Bret asked, breaking his thoughts.

"Yeah, I got some. Like you said, we've got to find us someone to rob."

"Yeah," Bret agreed.

The squaw put a big chunk of meat on a spit. Hailey still couldn't settle down. Something had to turn up—something to give them the money to buy their winter supplies.

"Someone's coming," Bret hissed, and gave a head toss to the south.

"One rider's all I see. Got two packhorses. She got any coffee made?" Hailey asked, looking back over his shoulder.

"Yeah, it's cooking."

"This may be our best chance. You follow me." Hailey walked toward the stream that separated them and the man on horseback.

"Howdy," the rider shouted. He had a repeater laid across his lap. A large-framed man, he wore a thick woven shirt the color of the brown grass. His once-gray unblocked hat was caked with sweat around the brim, and an eagle feather trailed from the hat band. His straggly black beard was untrimmed. He looked over the shallow cut, then booted his dun horse off the bank and his two packhorses followed.

"My name's Tabor Jennings." Jennings dismounted heavily in his Indian boots, then slung the rifle on the horn.

"Hailey Ketchem." He stepped up to shake the man's hand. "And that's my pard, Bret."

"Good to meet you, Bret." They shook hands.

"You boys ain't seen any buffalo, have you?" Jennings spat to the side, then wiped his mouth on the back of his hand.

"We killed three with some Cheyennes a day ago south of here. One got away."

"Sumbitch, there ain't any left. I guess I been riding for a week and ain't seen any fresh sign. Hate to go much further west. Them Cheyennes friendly?"

"Bret got that squaw from them."

"Not bad." Jennings licked his whisker-edged mouth as if taking her in while she busied herself bent over cooking.

"We got some buffalo to eat," Hailey said. "Turn your horses out. Sun's about to set."

"Mighty kind of you. I've rode a couple hundred miles from Chouteau's Post on the Vertigris, and ain't seen nothing but a bunch of damn foolhardy sodbusters. They ain't got the sense God give a goat. This ain't farmland, it's grassland. Couldn't tell them a damn thing."

Hailey agreed, and noticed the man carried a big Colt in his waistband when he sat down with them. The walnut stock stuck out like a polished plow handle from his belt. There were a couple of buffalo-skinning knifes on him. He could probably use them. They'd have to be careful taking him.

"What you two up to besides killing buffs with the Cheyennes?"

"We got us a stock ranch up in the brakes."

"Smart enough. Stupid bastards think they can plow up all of Kansas and Nebraska and plant it to corn."

"Yeah, but the Republicans didn't want them starving bastards picketing the White House. That's why Lincoln got that homestead act. Send them west, not to the capital, huh?"

"Yeah," Jennings agreed, as if for the first time he understood the flood of settlers moving like waves of invading locusts across the land.

"Ain't nothing going to stop them. Yankees won the war. They'll do what they damn well please for the next century."

"You're right," Jennings agreed. "I got some hooch I been saving. Ain't sure why, but you two would make someone good to share it with. Want a drink?"

"Hell, yes, we do," Hailey said, impressed at their good fortune.

"Sure," Bret said.

"Give that squaw a snort or two. She might do us some dancing." Jennings waved at her on his way to the pack-horses.

Hailey, seeing the resentment on his brother's face at Jennings's offer, quickly put his hand on Bret's arm to stay him. "A little squaw dancing won't hurt. Hear me?" he hissed.

"Yeah, what can it hurt," Bret finally agreed.

"Good," Hailey said, watching Jennings return with the crock jug.

Each man held out his tin cup for the hunter to serve him. Jennings filled his own, then turned and said something casual in Cheyenne to the woman. She looked up and then nodded.

Then she caught up her fringed skirt and ran over for him to fill hers too. She squatted down and held out the cup, saying a few words to him. Then she nodded at him, rose, gave a big grin to Bret, and went back to her cooking, sipping some on the way.

The liquor had a kick, and cut loose all the phlegm in

Hailey's throat. He had a coughing fit until tears squirted from his eyes and his breath drew short.

"Good stuff," he managed.

"Real mule-ass-kicking firewater." Jennings looked at his cup's contents as if he was reflecting on the matter, then took a good sip. He made a pleased "ah" sound. "Her name's Blue Flower."

"Bret calls her something else."

"Little red bitch like that in his blankets could make an old man's pecker hard as a hoe handle," Jennings said.

They chuckled at his words.

Hailey noticed the squaw began acting up some. She finally tossed down the last of the whiskey.

"Get you some more hooch, Flower." Jennings waved the jug at her in a circular fashion.

She came over, stumbling slightly on the way, and he refilled her cup. Then he asked her something else in Cheyenne, and she nodded.

"Then do it, girl," he said, making a circle with his free hand.

She giggled, straightened her spine, and pushed out her small breasts into the stained deerskin blouse. Then she shook her braids and head from side to side. With a smug look on her face, she began to sip down the liquor. Finished, she tossed the cup aside with a clank. Stomping her feet, she began to chant and sing. "Hey yoo, hey yoo."

The tune of her song rose and fell as she shuffled around the fire. The tempo soon grew faster. Never stopping her movement, she fought the blouse off over her head so it wouldn't impede the more complicated steps and arm tossing that made her small breasts shake. Her braids jerked like two limp snakes, and whipped around her bare shoulders with her motions. Hailey watched as her fingers plucked at the strings of her skirt.

Seated between them, Jennings threw out his arm and struck Hailey on the shoulder to get his attention. "Now she's going to do it stark naked,'' Jennings said, out of breath.

Taken aback by the blow, Hailey realized the man's intense concentration on her activities would give them a chance to strike. He watched Jennings reach down, grab himself, and resettle his crotch as if he had a cramping hard-on in his pants.

The copper moons of her tight ass were soon exposed to the campfire's light, and the dark triangle of her public hair shone raven black. She danced on, her chanting louder, more intense. Jennings shifted uncomfortably beside him, then reached inside his waistband and his hand stayed there.

Hailey eased his Colt out of the holster. He cocked it, and the sound caused Jennings to turn. The blast was deafening, and the hunter was slammed back by the concussion of the bullet in his face. Taking no chances, Hailey rose on his knees and pumped two more slugs into the man's chest. Except for the twisting of his right leg, Jennings made no more movement. His face, black from the powder blast, became a mask of blood from the hole in his forehead where the first bullet had entered.

Unsteady and shaken, Hailey rose with the smoking pistol in his hand. The naked squaw came to hang on to the stunned Bret, who looked in disbelief at the dead man.

"Scalp him and get his clothes off. I want that good shirt he's wearing," Hailey ordered. "Get the damn fire on it out.''

"I ain't never scalped no one.'' Bret looked at him in disbelief.

"You live with a damn squaw. Let her show you how.''

"Hell, what are we going to do with him?''

"Scalp him, strip him, and then dump him in that stream and make it look like Injuns done it.''

The squaw had used some camp water to slosh on Jennings. When the smoldering fire was out, Hailey holstered his Colt, bent over, and undid the man's belt and pants. Waving for her to help undress him, he straightened as she removed his boots. Then she pulled his britches off with some effort. Disgusted with the damage to the shirt, Hailey undid the buttons. There were bullet holes and blood all over it; he might not be able to save it to wear.

He looked around for Bret. His brother acted busy sharpening a large skinning knife with a stone.

"Hell, it don't need to be perfect," Hailey said, and glanced at the squaw, who looked entranced, staring down at the man's exposed genitals. Even in death, Jennings seemed hung bigger than his stud horse.

"Big one, huh?" he asked her.

She giggled and nodded in agreement. Then, with her arms full of clothes, she took them away.

"Jesus, I hate to scalp him," Bret protested.

"Give me the damn knife," Hailey said, filled with impatience. He had to do everything else, might as will scalp the sumbitch himself. He took the knife away, bent over, grasped the man's greasy long hair in one fist, and let out a scream as the razor-sharp blade scraped over the skull bone and the rug came off in his fingers.

All he could think about was Jennings's whiskey. He'd need more of it.

15

The sun hung low in the west and the crimson shafts speared across the prairie. In the deep, shadow-filled canyon below them nestled a set of lodgepole corrals and a small alfalfa field gone to purple blossom along a spring-fed ditch.

"Is that our land?" she asked, standing beside Slocum.

"This is the location." He considered the place much more valuable than he had expected. It held some good prospects as a place for the two of them to settle. The notion of its value made him wonder. Was someone already claiming it?

"There's a cabin down there." Jeremy pointed, riding up on his pony.

"We saw it. This may not be so bad after all," she said, looking relieved, and started back for the wagon.

"Jeremy," Slocum called out to him. "Hold up. There might be serious squatters down there. I better go ride down there and check it out. Tell your mother to wait until I give the signal."

"Yes, sir." He spurred his pony towards her.

Slocum swung up and sent his horse down the steep hillside through the cedars. Out of habit, he felt for, then undid the leather tie-down on his Colt's hammer. His senses grew more acute, wary of who might have moved into such an abandoned place. Folks took every opportunity to settle in when such a place had no obvious residents. In most cases the squatters were willing to fight for their digs, too.

Halting behind a log shed, he noticed a pair of britches on the line, flapping in the wind. His hunch proved right. There were residents. He drew his Colt and dismounted with care. Peering from the edge of the building, he could see the back door of the cabin was open. No windows in the rear. He hurried across the yard, ready to shoot it out or give warning.

With his shoulder to the wall beside the back door, he listened.

"Confounded boys ought to be back by now," an older woman's profane voice said, cutting the air. "They ain't worth a gawdamn anymore."

"Quit grumbling, Ruby, they'll—"

"Don't make a move," Slocum said, stepping over the threshold.

"Who the hell are you?" the woman demanded.

"I work for the lady who owns this place."

"Ha. They hung the owner last spring," the needle-nosed woman said with the beady glare of a setting hen in her black eyes. "It's our place now. I got a claim on it."

"No, you don't. His wife and son are taking possession."

"Too late. Our banker's done filed a claim."

"When?"

"Week ago, didn't he, Luther?"

"He sure did." The gray-headed man in the white shirt stuck his thin chest out with all the importance of a governor.

"You're both liars. I went to the land office in Ogallala yesterday and there isn't such a claim on record. Besides, you're too late."

"You ain't going to put an old woman out on the ground, are you?" She assumed a look of disbelief that he would even consider such a thing.

"You have thirty minutes to pack and leave peacefully.

I'll take that old blunderbuss and you can get it at the front gate.'' He crossed the room and took the double-barrel from beside the front door. The tall, thin man had already acted as if he might reach for it.

"Better get packing," Slocum said.

"The sheriff will hear about this!" she screeched at him.

"Already spoke to him, but go ahead."

She looked around, then began flinging her things into a carpetbag. "What is your name?"

"Slocum."

"Slocum? You ain't the Slocum from Dodge?" She narrowed her thin silver eyebrows at him.

"Texas. San Antonio."

"Yeah," she said, and shook her head in disapproval. "You ever been to Dodge?"

"Many times. What's it to you?" Slocum looked hard at her, but she shrugged off his question and busied herself gathering things.

"Someone's coming," Luther said, and went to look out the front door.

"Mrs. Brown and her son. Now get to packing."

"Brown never mentioned having a wife," she grumbled.

"Maybe you didn't ask," Slocum said, and with the shotgun held in his left hand by the barrel, he went out to explain his eviction plans to the Browns.

Dora and Jeremy listened to him, looking up as the man brought out things to put in the wagon.

"I hate to make old folks get out," Dora said, concerned.

"Take my word, they aren't helpless, and if they hadn't lied to me at the start, I'd have been more concerned."

"Do you think she knew him?"

"Acted like she did."

"I want to speak to her then."

Dora tied off the reins on the brake handle and climbed down, and Slocum could tell by the faraway look on her face that she was determined to speak with the woman. He walked a few steps behind her, in case hell broke loose.

The older woman was busy straightening things in the wagon, and looked up pained at Dora's words.

"Hello, I'm Dora Brown. You knew my husband?" she asked openly, approaching the rig.

"We worked for him some." Her eyes like coal chunks, she glared back at Dora.

"What did you do for him?" Dora asked.

"Took care of this farm and his stock."

"Where are they?"

"What?"

"His stock," she said, looking around for them. "I haven't seen any around here."

"Wandered off, I guess."

"Did you sell them?"

"That would be rustling. My man, Luther, is a man of the cloth, I'll have you know. We never took nothing wasn't ours. In fact you owe us for six months labor here."

"I don't see much you've done. Tell me what it was you did."

"You're a hateful hussy. We kept this place for him. Luther, get that horse hitched. I ain't taking her sass no longer." The woman mounted the wagon in a tiff and went to the front. Not looking back, she climbed on the seat as if they did not exist.

Slocum watched Dora's breasts rise and fall. Arms folded over them, she made a defiant picture staring, while Luther drew his stiff lanky frame up on the seat beside the huffy woman. Luther clucked to the horse. Slocum hurried up to the rig and stuck the shotgun in the back of the box.

"Why did he have someone like that working for him?" Dora asked.

"She was probably lying about that too. I'd say they moved in hoping to claim it."

Dora shook her head in disbelief. They watched the wagon on its way toward the end of the hay meadow. "We better get to work," Dora said. "It'll be pitch black in no time."

Slocum started for his horse.

"Thanks again," she called out to him.

"Yes, ma'am," he said over his shoulder.

"You aren't leaving us, are you?" she asked in a small voice.

Slocum shook his head and turned back to smile at her. "Just getting my pony."

"Good," she said, sounding enthused. "I'll have supper in a little while."

Slocum could hear the boy bubbling over about the place to his mother until he went out of earshot. It was a good location. The big spring made it double nice. The cabin was well chinked and looked dry. Brown must have had plans for the place. The alfalfa looked like a new plot, and while Slocum couldn't see it all, he suspected there were over ten acres of it under pole fencing.

He gathered his horse and started around the shed for the pen. His roan was with the colts. All his gear and packs were in her wagon to save packing and unpacking them off his horse. The smoke from her fire curled up his nose on the night wind. It would be a nice setup. Break some horses, winter some limpers, build up a cow herd.

Twilight deepened the shadows in the canyon. He removed the saddle, the heat and strong aroma of the horse's back touching his senses. Under the circumstances, he could never stay there with her and the boy. Still, it was nice to think about such a dream.

"You ever cut hay?" Jeremy asked when he joined him at the washbasin outside the back door.

"Some. Why?"

"There's a mowing machine in that shed over there. Shiny as new too."

"It's a wonder someone didn't steal it. Let's go see it before it gets plumb dark."

Slocum lit a match for light and squatted down on his boot heels inside the shed. He admired the new, long oak tongue, the black seat, and the row of teeth with the sickle sections under them so well oiled, they barely showed any sign of rust.

"Can we mow with it?" Jeremy asked.

"Yes, we can. It is a brand-new Dearing machine. One of the best, they say, on the market."

"How much hay can we make?"

"Sky's the limit, I guess." Slocum blew out the match and rose to his feet. "Looks like a real fine machine."

"We better go tell Ma."

"Right," Slocum said, listening to a distant howl of a coyote. Another answered. He paused to make sure the calls were from real coyotes. Then, in the dimming light, he hurried after the excited boy. *Yes, Mrs. Brown, we have a brand-new mowing machine for your alfalfa.*

16

An extra saddle horse, with the other two horses loaded with furs and plunder, would sure bring a pretty penny to tide them over. Hailey closely examined the dead man's .50-caliber Spencer repeater. Good weapon. If they'd had it on the buffalo hunt, his mare might still be alive.

"How much money you get off him?" Bret asked.

"Maybe a hundred dollars."

"Maybe?" Bret asked, pained at his answer.

"Hell, I ain't counted it coin by coin."

"You reckon someone finds his body they're going to think Injuns killed him?"

"They damn sure will. We used his barefoot horse to carry him over there, and the only prints in the mud were her moccasins."

"We better get our butts over to the hideout. Ma will be pissed anyway, it's took us so long to get up here."

"I ain't bringing in no damn squaw with me, am I?" The notion amused Hailey; he knew well her opposition to her sons taking Injun wives.

"I don't give a damn what she says. I'm keeping this one."

"Your ass, not mine." Hailey shoved the Spencer in the scabbard under his stirrup. The two packhorses would bring twenty bucks apiece. The gear, hides, and furs another fifty, maybe more. Jennings's saddle horse might be recognized, so they'd keep it to use or sell to someone on the run. Men on the run came by their place from time to time, and would need a fresh horse.

The squaw rushed about camp, finishing loading everything. Hailey studied the clouds building in the east. It was early in the day for such formations. They might get rain before dark. He hoped they were at the shack by the time the thunderstorms struck. A man could be hailstoned to death in one of those cloudbursts up here. He'd been beaten half to death before by ice balls as big as his fist.

With dread in his stomach over the possibility of such weather developing, he swung in the saddle and reined the paint around. Bret was taking a piss with his back to him, holding his reins in one hand. The squaw, with her fringe flying, lined up the other animals and her packhorse. Hailey set spurs to the paint. They could come on and catch up to him whenever they liked.

By late afternoon, they reached the brakes and were descending the trail off the rim. Hailey felt tired, his back and legs aching from the long ride. His mouth was dry, and he'd drunk the last whiskey the man had had in the saddlebags when the squaw and Bret weren't looking. It was none of their business anyway—he ran the outfit.

A wagon was in the yard, and a horse raised his head in the pole corral. Ma was there. Why wasn't she at the Brown place? Those papers were already supposed to be made up. Something had gone wrong, and she'd be mad as hell. Filled with dread, he dismounted heavily from the saddle and began to undo the girth.

"About time you lazy boys got your asses here," she said from the doorway. "Luther and me got ourselves evicted from that Brown place by that low-life dog Slocum, who shot my baby boy Arlie dead in the streets of Dodge. You got to go see about them papers. He promised us that place."

"How did Slocum get here so fast?" Hailey asked, amazed that the man had beaten them to Nebraska.

"Never mind how. He's here. Who's that with your brother?" she asked, ignoring Hailey.

"That's his new Cheyenne wife."

"I ain't having no gawdamn half-breed grandchildren." She stomped her foot.

"Howdy, Luther," Hailey said to the man, ignoring her and starting for the house.

"She can pack her ass out of here right now!"

"Tell Bret that; she ain't mine."

"I ain't having no diseased, red nigger whores around my place."

"She ain't a whore and she ain't diseased," Bret said. He dismounted and the argument was on between the two of them.

"You boys have much trouble getting here?" Luther asked, walking beside Hailey, acting anxious to avoid the pair's shouting argument over Bret's new mistress.

"Had some with Indians. Lost a good mare trying to fly over a ravine. It was hell. You two have any trouble?"

"Nope, we drove right up here, and then Slocum moved us off'n that Brown place. That gunman. The one caught you boys."

"I know the sumbitch that shot Arlie down. What about him?"

"He brought a redheaded woman up here he claimed was Brown's widow and her boy a day ago, and rooted us out of the place. I tried to get to my Greener, but he looked fast as lightning with that Colt."

"Suppose we ought to figure out how to run them off."

"That Slocum will stay there." Luther shook his head warily. "He's a tough nut. Won't be no easy task to run him off."

"Hey, we got rid of Brown, didn't we?"

"Yeah, but this Slocum is a real hardcase. I've seen his

kind before. Better not mess with him 'less you got him in your sights.''

"There's always a way." Hailey looked back. Bret still had his squaw, and the old woman was stalking back to the shack mad as a wet hen. Hailey turned his attention to the tall cumulus clouds and the lightning flashing in the towering pink-white clusters. He dreaded the next few days. Ma was mad at Bret over bringing that red slut home with him. Ma wanted Arlie's blood revenged too. That meant facing or backshooting this Slocum. Deafening thunder shattered his worries, and dime-sized hail began to pelt the ground like large rock crystals. The size of the hail increased; the roar of the wind and the storm's sounds grew ear-shattering. Inside the cabin, Hailey used his hands to muffle the sound. The squaw, Ma, and Bret all ran in through the front doorway.

After a half hour of pounding, the fury outside let up and the roof leaks slowed to drips. Hailey glanced up at the exposed shingle underside, seeing many wet spots. Either the hail or something had damaged them.

"Move that pot under it!" Ma screeched at him, indicating the kettle on the table. She meant for it to catch the stream that poured down close beside him.

"I ain't half as mad about Slocum as I am that man lied to you about fixing the claim on the Brown place," she said. "Why, that roof on that place don't leak at all. It's tight as a bull ass in fly time. You boys got to do something about getting that settled. That woman ain't a bad looker either. Hailey, you need to court her away from that Slocum. Sure would make—" She whirled around and scowled at the squaw. "You sure could make better-looking grandkids with her than your stupid-ass brother will with that red nigger." Ruby shook her head in disapproval. "Them kind are the first to stick too. Every time, drop your pants and they're pregnant."

Her bitching put him on edge. He began to wish they'd stayed with the smoke-stinking Cheyennes. The damn Indians didn't bitch as much as she did. He knew the instant it happened in Dodge that Arlie getting himself killed during that bank robbery would be something she would never forgive the two of them for for the rest of their lives. Plus, he needed to see about the claim on Brown's place that was supposed to have been settled months ago.

"Well, when you going after Slocum?" she asked, peering out the front door for any signs of another storm.

"He ain't ordinary. We need to go check him out."

"Well, what you waiting for?" she demanded.

"Ma, he can wait."

"No, he can't wait. He done killed my baby boy in cold blood, and I ain't sleeping till you two get revenge for that."

"Gawdamnit, I'll do something!" Hailey slapped on his weather-beaten hat and burst out the front door. Grateful to be escaping the sharp-tongued bitch's lashing remarks, he headed for the corral.

"And you, you lazy lout," Ruby said inside the shack. "Get your ass out of here and help your brother."

"I'm going, I'm going," Bret pleaded, driven outside by her slaps on his arms.

Hailey never looked back. He saddled his horse. The seat was wet and he tried to dry it on his sleeve so his butt wouldn't be wet the whole way. The paint's coat was dark from the rain. No matter, he was headed out of this place and away from her bitching. Good thing they had Jennings's money.

"Where we going?" Bret asked, booting his horse to keep up.

"Anywhere to get away from her." Hailey gave a scowl back towards the shack. She wasn't in sight.

"Yeah. We going looking for this Slocum?"

"We better go by Sam's store first. He'll know if they got any new posters out on us."

Bret looked over his shoulder, then turned back and shook his head.

"What's wrong?"

"I hate to leave that squaw back there when Ma's on the warpath."

Hailey agreed with a nod, then spurred the paint stud into a gallop. That squaw was no worry of his. He could see the cumulus clouds building again. More damn storms coming. They were gathering both in the south and west. Thunder closed in, and Hailey and Bret rode their sweaty horses down the draw and hitched them in the cedars. With an ominous eye over their shoulders at the approaching rain, they hurried to the half-sod, half-adobe structure on the hillside.

"Hey, boys!" Sam hollered from behind the bar. A flickering candle dimly lit the interior of the store and bar. One man, a big man, looked up mildly at them from where he leaned on an elbow with his drink.

"Good to see you, Sam," Hailey said, and shoved his hand out to shake the freckled, red-hair-covered paw of the burly saloon keeper.

"You boys been gone for a while."

"Yeah," Bret agreed.

"Where's the kid?" Sam asked with a quizzical look.

"Dead. A gunfighter got him in Dodge."

Sam frowned, leaned on the bar, and looked hard at them. "Who did it?"

"A fella called Slocum."

Sam paused as if in deep reflection, then slowly shook his head. "Never heard of him before."

"He took over the Brown place, Ma said."

"Took over the Brown place, huh?" Sam still seemed deep in thought.

"Yeah, he run her and Luther off there just a day ago." Hailey lowered his voice and indicated the other man at the bar. "Who's he?"

"Stranger. Cattle buyer, he says." Sam shrugged to indicate he had little information about the man.

Hailey looked over when the man took a sip of his glass of whiskey. Somewhere he had seen that face before—had it been in Dodge? He wasn't Slocum. Hailey would never forget *his* face. When Slocum stepped out from behind that cottonwood and leveled that rifle at them, that had been the start of the worst of times for Hailey and Bret—with Arlie already dead.

"Give us a good bottle of whiskey," Hailey ordered.

Bret agreed with a nod. "We need two of them. That old woman is harder than ever to get along with."

"Want two?" Sam looked undecided about their request.

"Yeah, one each," Hailey said, and dug out more money for the second one.

They retired to a side table. Hailey felt relieved that Sam hadn't mentioned anyone coming around there and asking about them. Maybe the news hadn't reached there yet about their fiasco in Dodge. Good. Hailey poured himself a half glass and toasted his brother.

"What we going to do about that Slocum?" Bret asked with a frown.

Hailey looked through the brown liquor at the flickering candles on the wagon wheel overhead. The light had a wavering glare through the liquid.

"Kill him," he said, and meant it.

17

The rain cleared out overnight, and diamond sparkles of water droplets shone on everything that greeted the morning's first light. Slocum rode up on the ridge to check the horizon, and the sky looked clear for a hundred miles. With no sign of anyone, he reined the horse around. He still had some time left to linger and help her and the boy. Time to cut some hay—the moisture would be dried off by mid-morning. That decided, he rode back to the house. He felt anxious about the haying operation as he washed his hands and face at the back door to get ready for breakfast. The aroma of her food was wafting out the open doorway.

"You think he bought that mower for this place?" she asked when Slocum came inside and hung his hat on the peg. A view of Dora's full-figured form standing at the stove made his empty stomach roil—lots of woman there.

"Must have," he said. "Those two we ran off never did much work ever in their lives."

"It's never been used?" she asked, looking at him with a frown.

"Not that I can tell. New as a baby."

"Huh. It must have cost a pretty penny."

Slocum agreed, and took a seat at the table. Her late husband obviously had made some money in his illicit business.

Probably why he hadn't sent for her and the boy—it would have been hard to explain to a wife.

"Can a team of those mules of ours pull it?" she asked.

"They might not like it, but they can pull it. We'll switch teams. Use each team a half day until they gain some weight."

"Jeremy, did you wash up?" she asked the boy when he came in the back door.

"Yes, ma'am." He held up his hands to show her.

"Get to your place and you better eat up—I think today is the day. If Slocum's ready?"

"Jeremy and I are both ready. We intend to make some hay today." He smiled at the boy, who bobbed his head with anticipation glinting in his eyes.

"My, my. I must say, this whole business is very exciting." She hurried off to get the rest of their breakfast on the table.

"We'll need to find a bunch rake," Slocum said, passing the youth the platter of soda biscuits.

"What will that cost?" she asked, taken aback by the new information. When the bowl of gravy was set on the table, she paused before tucking her skirt under her to sit down on the bench across from him.

"I'm not sure. I'll have to ride into Ogallala and find one."

"Oh. How much are they? I don't have—"

"I collected a long-over due sum of money in Dodge. I can advance you the money."

"But Slocum, how can we ever pay you back?"

He busied himself opening a steaming biscuit. "I ever need that rake, I'll come get it."

"We can't take your charity forever."

"Try it for a while," he said, and smiled at her.

She blushed, dropped her gaze, and shook her head. "Somehow Jeremy and I will repay you. But we'll sure need the rake if we stay anyway."

At ten o'clock sun time, he walked along behind the mower and drove the spooky mules with the lines. Obviously the clack of the machine had the pair scooting right and left to get a look at this new contraption that trailed them. The bridle blinders denied them the look they desired, and they were forced by his hands on the lines to do his bidding. He cautioned Jeremy about the dangers of the sickle bar. A man could lose a leg in an instant in front of one of them. The youth said he understood, and ran ahead to take down the gate poles to the sweet-smelling field.

At last in the knee-high greenery, Slocum dropped down the bar, engaged the gears, and took his place on the seat. He nodded confidently to Dora and Jeremy. At the cluck of his tongue, the apprehensive mules struck their collars at the same time. Heads high, at the first clack of the mower bar they both gathered up and tried to break and run. On the iron seat, his boots firmly braced on the crosspiece, Slocum hauled them down and spoke sharply to them. Their exaggerated walk caused the plants to quake and then fall mowed off behind the sickle bar. Filled with newfound confidence, he made the mules walk faster. The path behind left a three-and-a-half-foot strip of mown green hay like a ribbon. Once the initial shock was over for them, he knew the team would soon settle down.

Birds chirped at him, disturbed bees busy gathering pollen from the purple flowers buzzed over his head, and an occasional grasshopper flew by his face. The strong alfalfa aroma hung sweet and heavy on the wind. Each hour the day's heat rose, and the sweaty mules soon found a pace to handle the machine. He paused and let them blow after each long round. Dora brought him a cool drink from the spring, and Jeremy saddled his pony to join him.

"How much hay is out here?" she asked at one of his breaks.

"Tons," he said.

"We'll need it, won't we?" She squinted her green eyes against the sun and looked over the mowed portion.

"I suspect so."

"How will I ever repay you?" she asked him in a low

voice as she took the water jug back from him.

"Don't worry about that. I better get to mowing," he said, and pulled the team's heads up from grazing in the fresh-cut stems. "Get up, mules! Thanks for the drink."

"See you next round," she said. With small beads of perspiration on her face, she stood in the thick green mat and looked at him with confidence.

He drove the mules around the patch again. Already they realized where they had to be, and the outside animal made his path beside the uncut plants. The long trip from Texas had broken them. They would do her a good job for many years. He shut his eyes for a minute and savored the sound of the metal clacketty-clack of the machine's back-and-forth action over the ledger plates, slicing away the stalks and giving the land a haircut. Smart men figured out such machinery, but he compared it to a scythe. The machine was like a steamboat versus oars. The thought amused him, and he clucked to make the mules keep up.

Early afternoon, with half the meadow mowed, he drove the mules back to the lot.

"Quitting early?" Jeremy asked, riding up behind him.

"Yes, I need to go to Ogallala and find a rake."

"What can I do?" Jeremy asked.

"We'll pull the sickle bar out and you can take a flat file and resharpen it while I'm in town."

Jeremy looked disappointed at his suggestion, but nodded in approval.

Slocum rode the roan to town. En route, he made a mental list of things he needed: a box of sickle sections and some extra guards. Luckily he had not broken any. Also some rivets, a riveter, and ledger plates. He found them in the inventory at a blacksmith's shop. Then the big man shut down his bellows and forge to show Slocum the new rake around back. Wayne Toberman was the smithy's name, an authorized Dearing dealer. Under a coat of black paint, the eight-foot dump rake looked perfect. Made by the Harness Brothers in Toledo, Ohio, the device looked substantial. The man's price of thirty dollars sounded high to Slocum, but they finally settled on the rake and the parts he needed for the mower for that price.

"You going to get that home with one horse?" Toberman asked.

"May have to come back for it," Slocum said.

"Where are you haying at?"

"The Brown place."

The blacksmith said he knew the farm. "My boy will deliver it tomorrow for a dollar."

"Tell him come by noon and I'll give him a twenty-five-cent bonus."

The smithy grinned. "He'll be there before breakfast for that much."

"You sell Brown that mower?" Slocum asked.

"Yes. He planted that alfalfa last year and had plans to buy a rake like this."

"His widow is who I work for. What did you think about him?"

"Brown had enemies. Most of them he made himself."

"Oh. How did he do that?"

Toberman looked around to be certain they were alone, and stopped him before re-entering the low-walled shed. "Let's say he didn't play the game."

"I thought they said he raped a whore," Slocum declared.

"Why do that? She worked for him," Toberman said.

"Did he strangle her too?"

"Some folks believe that. Never was a trial, was there."

"You don't believe that, do you."

Toberman paused, looked inside the open back door to insure their privacy, then shook his head. "I think he made some folks mad. Important folks."

"There were other girls died strangely in his place."

"Hell, they all take that old Chinese pipe stuff. What do you call it? Opium. Most of them girls live pretty reckless lives. It's a short life anyway. You either marry some old boy or die young."

"If he didn't rape her and didn't strangle her, who killed her?"

"I don't know."

Slocum stopped, and the man halted again in the doorway. "Who got his money?" Slocum asked the man. "Obviously he was making plenty."

With a work-blackened hand, the man rubbed his chin in a circular pattern. "Ain't never heard. But you said it—obviously."

Slocum thanked the man, and led the horse across the street to hitch him outside the diner. The evening crowd had begun to gather in the eatery. He had to go to the back to find a place to sit at the counter. Tissie came with her order pad when he took a seat.

"You came back," she said under her breath.

"Yes, I've got more questions to ask you—later."

"Good," she said, and took his order.

Three hours later, he waited for her in the shadowy alleyway by her stairs. He listened to her speaking to someone on the boardwalk in front of the building that housed her place, and turned his ear to listen.

"Who's this fella making hay out at the Brown place? Been sneaking around at the land office asking all kinds of questions."

"How should I know? You're the law, Arnold, why don't you find out?" Tissie asked.

"Listen, bitch, I'll shove this .45 up you if you don't go to talking better to me."

Upset by his words, Slocum tried to see if the man was about to get physical with her. The best he could tell, it was only a verbal threat. Still, he undid the thong on the Colt's hammer. No telling what might happen next. He stayed back in the darker shadows and listened to them.

"Big man. So you've got a deputy's badge now," she said.

"Don't you act so highfalutin, bitch. You don't have a man to look after your butt anymore. You may need me.

There's some horny boys here in town might work your ass over without a man to look after you." Then he laughed as if the whole thing was amusing to him.

"Well, you'd damn sure be the last one I'd call on for help."

"Mind your mouth, woman, or I'll slap it shut."

Slocum couldn't see the man, but hot rage coursed his veins. This deputy needed a real lesson, and he was just the man to give him one. He clenched his fists at his sides. If the bastard hit her, he was ready to step out and deck him.

"Don't forget what I said, Tissie."

"Go to hell!" she said, then appeared at the alley's entrance and stalked to the bottom of the stairs. Slocum kept back in the shadows and waited. The lawman appeared also, but simply watched her go up the stairs and made no attempt to follow her.

"You bitch!" he swore, and turned, stopped a moment at the entrance of the alley between the two buildings, then shook his head as if in anger and stomped away. Slocum could hear his boot heels on the boardwalk going off.

"He's gone," she said in a half whisper from above.

"Yes." Slocum checked, then bounded up the stairs.

"That sumbitch!" she swore, then ushered him inside.

"Who is he?" he asked, and then recalled meeting him earlier in the sheriff's office.

"Deputy sheriff now. He just got that job given to him. His daddy owns the bank. A spoiled punk is what he is."

She crossed the room and stood at the window, looking down at the street to catch sight of the man.

"He still down there?" he asked her.

She stepped back and shook her head. With her hands she swept the hair back from her face. "You hear him threaten me?"

"Yes. He was asking about me."

"Yes."

"That's another matter. First, I've got some questions for you. You may not have liked Brown, but there are people here in town say he didn't rape that girl or strangle her."

"He did enough other mean things."

"Like what?"

"If you'd been here, you'd know."

"I wasn't here. Tell me what he did."

She hugged herself and coldly stared out the window at the street. He wondered if he had asked too much. Obviously she was not going to openly tell him. How could he ever find out the truth about the man? There were more unanswered questions all the time. Not a rape—not strangled—not tried in a court of law—lots of money gone—bank foreclosed on his whorehouse—a farm with alfalfa planted and a new mowing machine. The worst thing was, the man had been hung by vigilantes.

She wet her lips. "All right, I'll tell you what I know."

18

Winners and losers was how the world went. That was the way it looked to Hailey from his place in the chair at Sam's. He felt drunk, but he did some of his best thinking drunk. It kind of freed up his mind from other things.

"Slocum's at the Brown place," he muttered aloud, more to himself than Bret, who was already too drunk to do anything.

"You know Slocum?" the stranger from the bar asked.

Hailey looked at the man hard. He felt too drunk to be comfortable with him. Why didn't he mind his own business? Then the stranger put his freshly opened bottle of whiskey in the center of the table. "Have some."

Hailey nodded, and tried to consider the man's motives. He splashed some whiskey in his glass and motioned for the man to sit down.

"What's your game?" Hailey asked, trying to focus on him.

"That damn Slocum is wanted in Kansas."

"He is?" Hailey wondered what for. Back in Dodge, the sumbitch had acted like a cousin to the Earps.

"Fort Scott. They got a murder warrant out for him."

"So?"

"They got two special deputies on his trail all the time."

"How come you telling me all this?"

"He robbed me in Dodge."

"Robbed you in Dodge?" Hailey blinked his blurry eyes in disbelief at the man.

"Yeah, he claimed I owed him on a cattle deal, but I paid him that money two years ago in San Antonio."

"Why didn't you turn him in?"

"Ha. With him so tight with them Earps down there? Who'd believe me?"

"Right." Then the notion struck Hailey. Wire the law in Fort Scott. They wouldn't have to take a chance of messing with Slocum—let the law take its course. Who *was* this man? "I never caught your name."

"Rhodes, Johnny Rhodes."

"Hailey Ketchem. This here is Bret."

His brother raised up, offered a limp hand for the man to shake, then mumbled something about "nice" and put his face back down on the tabletop. "Ma ain't running her off," he mumbled.

"Don't mind him," Hailey said to Rhodes in disgust. "What's your business up here?"

"I need a set of cows for delivery to Montana. Know of any?"

"Give me a few days to think about it."

"A few hundred would sure help."

"I might could find that many," Hailey said, searching his memory. Cattle meant money and they needed lots of money. Didn't care how either—for the moment rustling looked a lot easier than bank robbing.

"Have some more whiskey," Rhodes said, offering him the bottle.

In his alcohol-twisted mind, Hailey began to see the answer to the problem with Slocum. Get word to the law in Fort Scott. "How much reward they *paying*?"

"Maybe five hundred," Rhodes slurred, and poured both of them another glass.

"You hear that?" Hailey blinked at his brother. The sumbitch was snoring facedown on the table. Big help he'd be in case he needed him. In defeat, Hailey slumped back in the chair. They'd get rid of Slocum. He grinned to himself, deeply engrossed in his plan to collect the reward.

"Hey, you know where there's some cows for sale?" Rhodes asked him.

"Yeah. Yeah, we'll find some for you." Hailey couldn't believe his good fortune. Reward money and get rid of that damn gunfighter. He closed his eyes and then jerked himself awake. He didn't dare go into Ogallala himself. No problem. He'd send in Luther and Ruby to notify the officials in Fort Scott.

"Where are them cows at?" Rhodes asked, breaking into his daydreams of success.

"Hell, I'll have to find them. What you paying?"

"What kind are they?"

"Hell, I don't know yet." Then Hailey broke into laughter. Damn, he and Rhodes were both drunk as hooters.

Hailey's head hurt like a busted watermelon when he woke up. He'd slept in the shed out back of Sam's store. The hay had some kind of itchy weeds in it, and he couldn't scratch enough. The drum playing on each side of his head sounded louder than a Cheyenne war party. Unsteady on his feet, he used one hand to brace himself on the door facing, and squinted at the fiery red sun. Be another hot day. He needed to ride back and send Luther to town. Soon as he got that done, he could sit back and wait for the reward.

How long would it take the law to get there? A day or so. Less than a week. He squeezed his sore eyelids shut. Damn, his belly was on fire and he had to piss bad. With his shoulder to the wall for support, he emptied his bladder in the weeds beside the sod wall. Finished, he shook his tool, put it back, then rebuttoned his pants. Maybe Sam had some food fixed. He thought he saw smoke coming out of the store's stovepipe.

He went to the back door and peered inside. "You up, Sam?"

"Yeah, come in. You boys sure got drunk last night." The big man was busy cooking something, and the aroma sent Hailey back outside. His stomach rejected the smell, and he stood braced against the soddy wall and had the dry heaves until his eyes squirted water.

"You all right?" Sam asked, concerned, from the back door.

"Yeah," Hailey managed. "Need a drink to settle me."

"I'll get you one." And Sam disappeared.

His hands shaking so bad he feared he would spill the contents of the half-filled glass the big man gave him, Hailey drew it to his mouth. Some slipped by his lips, some ran off his chin, but the sharp liquor loosened the phlegm in his throat. That sent him off on a wave of coughing, and if Sam hadn't quickly taken the glass, he'd have spilled it.

At last, out of breath and defeated, he heaved for more air and tried to straighten up.

"Whew!" he managed, and took back the drink. In two gulps he managed to swallow the balance.

"You going to be all right?"

He looked into Sam's concerned eyes. "Yeah. I'll be fine now."

"Your brother and that cattle buyer—they still out in the shed?"

"I guess so. Didn't know how we got there."

"I helped you."

"Yeah, well, thanks. I owe you."

"You sober enough to talk now?" Sam searched around as if he wanted to be certain that they were alone.

"Sure, I'm fine." Hailey used his fist to pull down his shirt, and tucked in the tail with the flat of his hand. What did Sam want?

"There's someone been asking lots of questions about *him*."

"Him?"

"Brown," Sam said in a whisper.

"So? He's dead. We know that. Dead men don't talk."

"You know Brown had a widow?"

"Yeah, I heard about that. Run Ma and Luther off the place."

"I never heard about *that*. But this stranger was at the land office asking all kinds of questions a few days ago."

"Never mind, I got him handled," Hailey said smugly. "He won't be troubling us long."

"How's that?"

"Trust me. You can tell the others he will be out of here on his way to jail in no time."

Sam shook his head in disbelief. "You want some fried side meat?"

"Yeah, think I can eat now." Hailey swallowed hard. He hoped he could keep it down. He would need all his strength to ride back to the shack and get his plan in operation. Better do it quick too.

"What about them other two?" Sam asked when they finished their meal.

"Feed them when they get up, but make Bret stay sober. Tell Bret to get back to the place. Right now I've got to get things going so we can get rid of Slocum."

"That's this fella's name?"

"Yeah. You met him?"

"Nope, but I'll feel a lot better when he's out of here."

"Trust me," Hailey said, rising to his feet and pushing out his chest. "I'll handle this." He left the store and hurried to locate his horse. Seeing the paint far out on the prairie, he started for him.

The animal trailed broken reins and ate grass through the bits. Obviously it had been saddled all night, but had broken loose and gone about its business. Hailey found some rope in his saddlebags to use as reins.

He swung up and headed the paint for their hideout. No

sign of Bret or Rhodes; they must still be sleeping in the hay shed. He hurried the stud southwestward. No time to waste. He needed Luther on the way to Ogallala to inform the law. Things were smoothing out.

19

"When Brown opened the place, he must have heard one of the girls say something about me," Tissie began. "I'd worked in one of them back in Abilene before I got married. Brown knew I was having to work at the diner to make a living. He kept coming around telling me I should move in and how easy it would be up here.

"I hated the sumbitch. He never gave up asking me either." She shook her head and her eyelids narrowed. "I swore I'd never do that again even if I starved. Ain't nothing easy in one of them places. Rutting grubby old boars that come in there all the time—I can still smell the liquor on their bear breath, and they ain't had a bath since before they wrote the Bible." She gave a visible repulsive shudder of her shoulders.

Slocum nodded soberly and waited for her to continue.

"He never took no for an answer," she continued. "Kept coming by and saying how good it would be for me. I saw things. Girls died in his place. They took them out the back door late at night in a pine box, then quickly buried them in secret by coal-oil light—no preacher, no headstone, nothing!"

"You think he killed them?" he asked.

"Someone, something killed them."

"Might have been too much opium. Consumption?"

"I don't know. If he'd left me alone—" She shook her head to dismiss it. "I wasn't going back to that life. Not ever." Sorrow soon overcame her and she began to sob. "I hated him. He kept asking me to go back. I'm glad he's dead!"

"Did they kill him for what he did to some girl, or did they just kill him?"

"I don't know, Slocum. I don't know." She crumpled to the floor and began sobbing on the side of the bed.

"Did he ever physically threaten you?"

She raised up, her eyes flooded with tears. "No, but he kept—" She couldn't go on.

"Sounds strange to me. If he didn't rape that girl and there was no one to testify he strangled her, I guess a real court of law would have let him off."

"What are you getting at?"

"I want to know why someone or some people wanted Brown out of the way so bad they lynched him."

"You think they murdered him?" She snuffed her nose, then blew it on the kerchief he gave her.

"I think he either knew something or was in someone's way. The man at the blacksmith shop thinks the same thing."

Wearily she rose up and sat, dejected, on the edge of the bed. "It has to start with the banker, Jeremiah Arnold. He runs the town."

"His boy was that new deputy."

"Yeah, Joe. Had to find him work, he's too thickheaded to count money."

"Why would a banker want Brown out of the way?"

"Beats the hell out of me, Slocum."

"Who would know?" He walked back and forth across the room. "There was some old couple squatted on Brown's place. His name was Luther."

"That's the Ketchem boys' mother and stepfather. Arlie, Hailey, and Bret."

"I know them. Arlie got gunned down in Dodge a week ago, and the other brothers were jailed there for bank robbery. They broke out too."

"I'll be damned." She seemed taken a back. "They were there that night."

"The night they hung Brown? They were there? Who else?"

"They all had masks, but I recognized the oldest Ketchem's voice. The whole bunch was liquored up like they'd worked up their nerve from a bottle to hang him."

"Most mobs do that."

"What can you do about it now?"

"I don't know, Tissie. I have to go put up some hay, but keep your ears open for me."

"You have to leave so soon?"

"Yes."

She rushed over and hugged him. He held her tight for a long moment, then disengaged himself. No time for pleasure. Not if there was some way, maybe, that he could clear a dead man's name and bring his murderers to trial. He felt better going down the stairs in the dark. At the alley, he looked back. She had turned out her lamps, and in the starlight stood on the top step and waved.

He hurried toward where the roan was hitched. A half block away from the animal, his instinct told him to circle around. Colt in hand, he pressed himself to the rough-cut siding of the store building and studied the hip-shot gelding in the darkness. Asleep, the horse snorted softly, and Slocum tried to pick out anything out of the ordinary. He waited. Then the flare of a match gave away the sentinel across the street. For an instant in the match's light, Slocum even made out the scattergun the man carried in his arm.

Rule number one, you don't light a smoke on guard duty. Slocum eased back and circled the building so he could come up from behind the person. In the darkness, he found two empty whiskey bottles in the trash. Then stealthily, he moved to the narrow passageway between the two stores where the guard was standing.

He dared look up the passageway, and in the shadowy light he could make out the guard's outline up near the end. He went around the building to the west, crept across the porch that was used for a dock, and carefully drew himself up until he was within a few feet of where the man hid out of sight.

Slocum reared back and tossed the first bottle in the air so it would land in the passageway behind the guard. The bottle clattered off the roof and the blast of both barrels of the man's shotgun shattered the night. Dogs began to yelp and bark. In four steps Slocum was there behind the man and shattered the second bottle over his head.

His knees buckled, he dropped the double barrel, and then the unsuspecting lookout fell face-down. Slocum kicked the shotgun under the store building. Then he rushed for his roan. He wasted no time riding out of town. To leave them less of a trail, he avoided the ferry and made a wet crossing of the shallow river. No matter. From there on, his time spent in Ogallala would have to be under secrecy. That would hinder him even more. Upset with the knowledge, he loped the roan for Dora's place.

He dismounted heavily at the corral. A pink rim touched the horizon—not much time left before daylight to sleep. He tossed his saddle on the top rail and closed his dry eyes for a moment. There was hay to mow, and the rake would be there by midday. He spread his bedroll out on the old hay in the shed, shucked his boots, and lay down in his clothing. Quickly, he fell asleep.

He awoke as the sun streamed in the door. She squatted beside him with a cup of coffee.

"Took a long time to find a rake?" she asked.

He sat up and rubbed his eyes. "That and some other business."

"Oh, you did find a rake?"

"A boy is bringing it out here this morning."

"How much did it cost?"

"Thirty dollars, and that included replacement parts we'll need for the mower."

"We decided to let you sleep. Jeremy is mowing."

"Damn, how long did I sleep?" he asked.

"Never mind. We knew you came back late in the night. Besides, he needs to be confident he can do those things while you're still here."

"Yes," Slocum agreed.

"Come to the house. I have some biscuits and beans for you."

"Biscuits and beans. That's what the army lives on," he said, pushing himself up with some effort.

"About all we have left to eat."

"Get the hay up, perhaps we can find a buffalo for your winter meat supply."

"Oh, Jeremy would love that."

"There's some left somewhere on the prairie." Outside the shed, Slocum stood on his toes and watched the boy go by on his round with the mules. He could hear the clack of the machine, and nodded in approval, then headed for the cabin with her.

"He'll be all right, won't he?" she asked.

"Yes, the mules are used to it now."

"I thought so, and he worked so hard sharpening that sickle bar after you left, I couldn't turn him down when he asked."

Slocum agreed, and stopped at the washbasin to scour his face and hands. She handed him the small sack towel to dry with.

"Dora, things may get tight for me here and I may not be able to stay with you and him much longer. I want you to keep a gun handy. There's something out of place and I haven't sorted all of it out yet."

"Like what?"

"Someone with a shotgun was waiting to shoot me last

night in town. Seems I've asked too many questions about your late husband, his land ownership, and his money."

"Who is behind it?"

"Better you didn't know for now. I'm not certain, but there are some worthless outlaws involved, for one thing."

"Who's that?"

"The Ketchem gang. It was their mother and stepfather we ran out of here."

"But she said they worked for my husband."

"There's more here than either of us know right now. I'll get to the bottom of things, but I may have to lie low to do it."

"Slocum. Be careful. I don't expect you to get hurt for Jeremy and me."

"I don't intend to get hurt. But you be on your guard and the two of you stay close together."

"Did you learn anything else?"

"Yes. I think the lynching was some sort of a cover-up."

"For what?"

"I don't know, Dora. I may never prove a thing, but for right now I have some leads."

"What can I do?"

"Put up hay for the winter with Jeremy. Oh, yes, you will owe that boy that brings the rake out this morning a dollar and a quarter."

"Kind of a steep price, isn't it?"

"No." He put the change to pay the boy on the table and shook his head. Then he sat down and began to fill his plate. He'd missed some meals since the last one. Maybe before things grew too tight for him to stay in the area, he could learn the real reason behind the hanging of her husband.

"Slocum."

He looked up at his name; she chewed on her lower lip under her even teeth. Something troubled her, and she made an effort to speak at last.

"You will come back and see us—I mean, me?"

He agreed. His stomach churned at the thought of her ripe body. At long last her veil of rigid resistance had cracked, and he had neither the time nor the place to take advantage. Yes, he would be back, Glendora Brown.

20

"Where did you leave that stupid Bret?" Ma demanded when Hailey dropped from his horse.

"He's coming behind. Luther, hitch that horse up to the rig. You've got to go to town and wire the law in Fort Scott, Kansas. They want Slocum for murder there, and they have a big reward and we'll be rid of him."

"Why, hallelujah! Praise the Lord! A reward even!" She threw her arms around Hailey and hugged him tight, then began putting wet kisses on him. "You are surely my smartest offspring. Don't stand there with your thumb in your ass, Luther. Go hitch that horse. We're going to be rich after all.

"How much is the reward?" she asked Hailey.

"Maybe five hundred."

"And we'd be rid of him! Maybe you could honey up to Brown's widow and we all could move back over there since the other deal didn't work."

"What's she like?"

"Good-looking. A little busty for my taste, but you men like that. Sure beats that trash Bret drug in."

"Where is she?" Hailey asked, looking around for the squaw.

"I didn't kill her yet. She's washing clothes out back.

Damn, I'd sure hate to have a damn half-breed grandchild.''

"Go easy. Bret will get tired of her in time.''

"I hope so. How long you figure it will take that law to come get that Slocum?''

"Week, ten days.''

"I'm going with Luther to town. He might lose his way. You got any money?''

"A little change is all.'' He sure didn't want her to know about all the Jennings money he had in his purse. From his pocket he produced four well-worn silver dollars and gave them to her.

"You're a good boy, Hailey Ketchem.'' She patted his whiskered cheek with her free hand. "How did you get this money anyway?'' She opened her palm to examine it.

"Off a dead Injun,'' he said, recalling the whipping she'd once given him for lying about money he'd held out on her. The skin on his butt drew up at the notion of her doing that to him ever again.

"The sumbitch must have had them for a long time. Damn near wore them out.'' She closed her long, thin finger on the coins, then stashed them away down the front of her blouse.

Hailey was relieved when she hitched up her skirt and headed off to join Luther. He felt better too that she had not noticed his shortness of breath. He'd been damn close to being discovered holding out on her.

With the two of them on their way, he went in the house to find some food. His upset stomach was still on fire. Shame they didn't have a cow. Some sweet milk might settle it. He found some leftover cold biscuits, and went to spreading some molasses on them. They were so dry they caked up in his mouth, and he tried to draw enough saliva in to swallow them.

The coffee left in the pot smelled bitter. With his mouth still full of the dry bread, he tried to drink from the dipper. Finally he managed to get it all down.

Then he saw the squaw standing in the doorway. Where

in the hell was Bret? He made a final swallow with some effort, and indicated with his thumb that his brother was coming. She nodded and disappeared. Good.

He heard horses, and went to look out the front door. It was Bret. His brother and the buyer Rhodes rode in together. They both dismounted heavily, and the squaw, with her fringe whipping, came running around the shack to meet Bret.

"Time you fellas showed up," Hailey said.

"Hell, what we got to eat?" Bret said with his arm around the woman.

"All I found was some dry biscuits like to choke me to death."

"Get some buffalo meat out and cook it, girl," Bret said, making signs and talking at the same time.

She nodded, and Bret slumped to the ground as if unable to go any further. He held his face in his hands and moaned as if in pain. "Damn, my head hurts."

"Hell, you're the one drank so much," Hailey said.

"Those cattle you spoke about?" Rhodes reminded him.

"I have to go see a man about them. What will you pay for them?"

"Ten bucks for a cow and big calf. I don't want no steers, they ain't bringing nothing. Them calves are small and can't be trailed, I don't want them."

"I understand."

Rhodes blinked his eyes and looked around. "Hell, you ain't got any cattle here."

"I said I would see the man about some."

"What man?"

"None of your business. You need cows and I got the man can get them."

"Not no rustled stock," Rhodes protested, as if shocked anyone would consider it.

"No. You'll buy them off a ranch around here."

"Good. When?"

"I've got to go see that man tonight. Rest easy, Bret's squaw's gone to fix some food for us."

Hailey had a special man in mind to see. If anyone in the country had cows for sale, he had them. Might have to conveniently foreclose on them, but Arnold always had folks whose notes were overdue at the bank and he held the mortgage on their herd. After what he heard cattle were being given away for in Dodge, ten bucks a pair might warm that banker's heart.

The morning passed slowly. They loafed around the front of the shack, and Hailey could smell the squaw's fire and cooking. At last, she brought each of them a large slab of brown-roasted buffalo. Hailey found a seat in the shade of the shack to sit on the ground and enjoy it. The grease and juices ran from the corner of his mouth when he bit off a bite. Nothing beat good meat.

Luther and Ma hadn't come back by sundown. Probably spending his four dollars. Hailey saddled Jennings's big stout horse. The dun was fresh and he had some riding to do. His plan was to ford the river and circle around Ogallala. This way he could approach Arnold's house under the cover of darkness and not be seen by hardly a soul.

His plan went smoothly. Hailey worried that Arnold might not be home, but when he saw the lights in the living room windows, he felt confident the man was there. He rode the horse around to the stables and put him in an empty stall, then went quickly to the dark back door.

He rapped softly and waited.

"You better not be no begging bum," a black woman said, undoing the latch. "Who you be?" she demanded, blocking the whole doorway with her ample form.

"Tell him that I need to talk to him," Hailey said in a whisper.

"Hmm," she snorted. "I don't know he even want to see the likes of you."

"Tell him!" Damn her, he'd slap her fat face in another minute. She needed to know her place.

With a "humph" she went waddling off through the kitchen, muttering to herself about the trash that came to her back door. He waited inside the open doorway.

"What's wrong?" Jeremiah Arnold asked, crossing the room and looking around to be certain there was no one with him.

"I've got a buyer wants two hundred cows and big sucking calves. He's talking about paying ten bucks a pair for them."

"Hmm." Arnold squeezed his goatee in his hand and considered the news.

"The market at Dodge is down to five dollars for steers."

"I know. It may get much worse too. If I get a herd, can we trust him enough to, say, pay eight and you get fifty cents and I get a dollar-and-a-half commission per head?"

"No problem." Hailey grinned as they stood on the dark back porch. The dull light from the kitchen spilled out on the flooring beside them. Arnold knew how to make deals. "He'll do it. He wants some cows bad enough."

"Good. Who's this person at the Brown place?"

"Glad you asked. He's a gunman and he's wanted in Fort Scott for murder. I sent word to the authorities today that he was here, and he won't be around long."

"Should I send Joe out to arrest him?"

"No. He's plenty tough. I'd let Fort Scott handle him."

"Good idea. We sure need to keep this Brown thing buried."

"I know that. Why I got the law coming for him."

"You did good, Hailey. How about a drink to celebrate that sale?" Arnold asked, sounding elated with the cattle deal.

Hailey felt he had done all the right things. He could sure use the hundred bucks the deal would bring him. Working with Arnold wasn't so bad after all. The man returned from inside and handed him a drink. He tasted it. Good whiskey. He drew a deep breath. Why, they'd been fools to go off down there and try to rob that bank in Dodge. They should have stayed home and worked on deals with men like Arnold. The whiskey slid down his sore throat like velvet.

"I know—I know," Arnold said hesitantly, looking around. "But I promise she'll get the Brown place when we get rid of this Slocum."

"Good enough." He'd almost forgotten about the land deal.

Hailey felt so good, he wanted to go into Ogallala and try the whorehouses. The more he thought about it, the harder he became. Should be some new girls in there by this time. Who was it who ran that place for Arnold? Sooie Claims. Big fat gal in her thirties who had watermelon-size breasts and pink skin. She could out-laugh anyone he ever saw. He loved to watch her big belly and tits shake when she was tickled. But it was safer if he went back to the shack and hid out until the Dodge deal blew over.

He returned the empty glass, shook Arnold's soft hand, and went to the barn for his horse. Arnold promised to send word when the cattle were ready. He better go straight back and tell Rhodes to get ready, that his partner would have those cows rounded up in the next few days.

But what the hell, it must be past midnight. Hailey reined the horse toward Sooie's place. With his gelding safe in the stables out back, he crossed the dark yard and studied the rooms with lamps on in them. Things might be slow in the middle of the week. He found the back kitchen door open, and two black women looked up from the table.

"You ain't suppose to—"

He held a finger up to his mouth to silence them. "You go tell Sooie I'm here."

"This ain't the damn parlor, this be the kitchen," the thinner woman said under her breath, getting up and going to get her.

Sooie soon came in the room, spotted him, rushed over, and threw her arms around him. With her full figure pressed to him, he felt his face grow bright red.

"Where have you been, baby? I haven't seen you forever,

darling. Come in here and pick you a nice a girl.''

He held back. She frowned at him and then smiled, waiting for his story.

"See, I got in little trouble in other places and everyone don't need to know I'm here.''

She reached over and pinched his cheek between her thumb and forefinger. "Well, Gawd almighty, you get your ass upstairs to the second room on the right. I'll send you up some sweet thing and you can fiddle with her all night for two bucks.'' She held her hand out for the money.

He paid her, glad he'd decided to come there. A stout whiff of her lilac perfume tickled his nose, and he thought he would sneeze. Somehow he held it. She gave him a big wink, then left the room shaking her broad fanny like a mare in heat.

Who would she send up for him? He wondered if he would be able to contain himself to even do it with her. Half sick to his stomach with concern, he climbed the stairs and slipped into the room unseen. A single candle burned on the dresser, casting his shadow on the walls. He took a seat on the bed and toed off his boots. The aroma of his sweaty socks, feet, and boots soon filled the room. He opened the window to air it out. He did not have long to wait.

The doorknob turned, hinges creaked, and a small face looked around inside for him. Then a wide smile crossed her red-stained mouth. The girl called Fantasia came prancing in wearing a sheer pink robe.

"Why, howdy, Hailey,'' she said in a full voice.

"Hush,'' he said, holding his finger to her mouth. "Ain't no one's business I been here.''

"Sure, fine, but where you been?'' She stood between his knees close enough that he could smell her musk and slight perfume. Better than campfire smoke and the smell of a damn horse like that squaw in Gray Wolf's camp.

"Seeing some country,'' he said, undoing the tie at her waist, opening the gown in the middle, and staring at her naked body.

He felt her small, globe-shaped breasts. She settled in his lap and tossed her light-colored hair back from the side of her face.

"There's two bounty hunters downstairs."

"There is! I mean, there is?" He lowered his voice. "Who do they want?"

"Some guy called Slo-dum."

"Slocum," he said, and moved her off his lap. He stood up and went to the window. Damn, there were bounty men already here for him.

"What's wrong?" she asked, slinking her body up against his leg.

"Nothing. I've got to think a minute."

Her fingers molded over the rise in his pants and she purred in his face. "Aw, honey, you're ready, all right."

Damn, them bounty hunters were already there.

"I'll be right back," he said, and began to put on his boots.

21

Evening settled in. Slocum's arms and shoulders ached deep when he tossed the last forkful of alfalfa on the wagon. Time to quit for the day.

He drove the pitchfork's tines deep into the sweet-smelling hay. Glendora walked along beside the rack with the leather lines to the horses in her hand, and tossed her head to move the curl of stray hair from her face.

"I never thought those cow ponies would stand pulling a hay rig," she said with a grin.

"Why not?" he asked, and took the lines from her to drive them back to the yard. The mules were worn out from mowing, so he'd hitched up the cow ponies and after a few rambunctious moves, they'd settled into hauling the hay from the field to the stack.

She quickly slipped in front of him and blocked his way. He was forced to rein them up, and she stood before him with her full lips pursed for him. He kissed her hard on the mouth.

"'Cause they were like cowboys, not made for farm work," she said at last when they came up for air. Her firm figure was pressed to him, so close she made his stomach roll at the prospect of having her body.

"This is dangerous," he said softly.

She wrinkled her pert nose and then lowered her eyelids. "I'm not afraid."

"Maybe you should be."

"Slocum, you've already done more for me than I could expect of anyone."

"I may not be here when the sun rises, too."

"I know. Maybe that's why I would like to repay you—with something."

He held the horses back. With his boot heels planted in the ground, he studied her full figure and then drew a deep breath. He wanted her. He'd wanted her since the first day he'd laid eyes on her in Kansas. But what price would they pay? He knew that every encounter had a cost. He didn't mean the work he'd done for her—what was the price for him to pay to at last have her body and soul?

"Can we take this load back and park it?" he asked.

"Of course," she said, and fell in beside him. "I have been thinking all day—about us." She reached down, drew up a long stem of grass with a seed head on the end, and began to taste it. "How we could hide you out here."

"You don't understand." He drove the horses through the gate with some care. He and she went ahead, and the edges of the load barely cleared the gate posts, but with a minimum of loss of hay it squeezed through the opening. With the load inside, they went for the house, the team straining in their collars to haul the load up the incline.

"There are men looking for you," she said.

"Yes, and they won't give up."

"Not even if we hid you so well they couldn't find you?"

"I couldn't let you and the boy face their wrath."

"I am not easily shaken."

"I know, but these men are cruel and stupid. They might hurt you or Jeremy if they even thought you stood in the way of capturing me. I can't take the chance."

"Slocum?" she said, sounding exasperated.

"Yes."

"I sent Jeremy off to town on an errand two hours ago so you and I—I—we could be alone."

"Why didn't you say so? How long do we have?" He bent over and unhitched the singletree, the whole time talking softly to the two horses.

"A while. He went to town for some baking powder and flour. Best excuse I could find."

"I am awfully sweaty and covered with hay," he warned her.

"There is water in the tub behind the house. I drew it this morning. It should be warm enough to bathe in."

"You can go first. I'll unhitch and be there."

"Don't be long." She kissed him and then ran for the cabin.

He drew a deep breath. No sign of anyone. He busied himself unharnessing the two cow ponies. The roan and bay made a good team. In a short while they would make regular workhorses. Free of their leather confines, they rolled in the dust, and he left them loose to graze.

With a wry look at the rick piled high, he realized it still had to be unloaded. There was lots of pitching left to do. But he had other things on his mind. The very thought of her full figure in his arms made his heart run faster and quickened his steps into a run.

He came around the corner of the cabin, anxious to jump in the tub and wash. She started at his approach, and darted inside the house with the towel only covering a small portion of her untanned flesh.

"Sorry," he said, stripping off his clothing.

"No," she said from inside. "I am not as brave as I thought I would be—don't be long."

"I won't," he promised, toeing off his boots, and in a short while stepped naked into the tepid water. He found the soap and lathered himself, then quickly rinsed off with a pail of water sitting beside the tub. Standing up and letting the water rush off, he searched for a towel.

"Here," she said from the doorway, and tossed him one.

He thanked her, noting she wore a flannel nightgown that hugged her form. When he looked up again she was gone. In a flash, he finished his drying and with the towel around his waist, tiptoed to the threshold.

"Do I need clothes?" he asked. His eyes were not accustomed to the dark room, and he wondered where she was at. Then she stepped into his arms, and with her palm swept the damp hair back from his face.

"Silly, what do you need clothes for?" she asked, nestling her naked form against him.

"Damned if I know."

Their mouths met and they soon caught fire, taking their breath away. Then his lips traced down her silky skin until he dropped on his knees and began to taste her rock-hard, dollar-size nipples. She clutched his head to them and cried out in anguish. "Oh, yes!"

At last, he rose and swept her shapely naked form up. With her in his arms, he started across the room for the bed bathed in the shadowy light. Like a feather he laid her on the bed. The fury of their rising passion blazed through his veins and thoughts.

He knelt on edge of the bed. With a knowing look on her face, she raised her pearly legs, parted them, and held out her arms for him to enter her gates. Like a swift storm, he came through the passage and situated himself. Using his left hand, he nosed his turgid shaft toward her wet gates, then braced himself above her. He could feel her body trembling from head to toe in anticipation of his entry. She raised her flat belly up to receive him, and slowly he began to enter her.

The soft cries of pleasure from her throat sounded desperate. Her sharp fingernails dug into the flesh of his upper arms. Slocum began to seek her depth with a slow but hard effort. He was barely halfway inside her ring when she briefly collapsed under him. Shaking off her dizziness and urging him on, she acted drunk as he sought more and more of her. Again she half fainted, and he smiled at her. Few women found such rewards so easily. Obviously she enjoyed it, for she drew him down on her breasts and raised her butt up off the bed for his last inch to penetrate her.

He began to pound her, and the friction of their lovemaking drew cries of "yes, yes" from her. Their pelvic bones ground together. His scrotum beat a tatoo on her tight butt with each pump. Their world turned inside out. His erection swelled harder and larger with each move. At last the skin on it felt ready to burst, and the nose of his dick burned and throbbed in pain from the swelling pressure inside. He reached under her, grasped both cheeks of her hard butt, and shoved himself as hard and deep as he could into her.

The explosion rose from deep in his balls and flew out the head of his dick like a rocket. They both gave anguished, strained cries at the final result, and fell in a helpless heap still connected. Slocum tried once to get up, but fell back in an unconscious state. They both slept for a while.

"Jeremy will be back any minute," she hissed in his ear.

He reached up, catching her glorious full head of hair in his fingers, and pulled her mouth down to his. Their lips met and the honey flowed. Then, like two drunkards, their faces parted.

"I'll get dressed," he said, then wondered where he would find the strength.

At last clothed and seated at the table, he considered the coffee and food she had prepared. The sounds of a horse coming hard made him reach for his Colt in the holster. They shared a concerned look with each other. He rose and went to the door.

Jeremy bound off his lathered horse and rushed to the door. "Slocum, two men called Abbott are in town and they're looking for you."

"Did you see them?" He searched the night and listened. Had anyone followed Jeremy back from town? Nothing out there he could hear or see, only the crickets chirping.

"No, but I heard them talking about it in the store," Jeremy said.

"What'll you do?" she asked.

"Move out now," Slocum said with a scowl. "Not one thing else to do."

"We'd hide you."

"I told you the answer to that."

"Come in and eat your meal. Jeremy can tell us all about them while you eat."

"I want to hear all of it," Slocum said. "I'll go put his horse up while he washes up."

He waved aside the boy's protest that he would do it, and took the reins and led the animal to the corral. Actually, he needed the time alone to sort out and think about what he had to do next. Still breathing hard and blowing, the boy's horse trailed him to the pen.

Slocum studied the thousand stars overhead while undoing the girth. Lord, he hoped his presence wouldn't endanger the two of them. They had a small hold on this ranch, but a cheating lawyer and some paper shuffling could take that away from them. How could he insure they kept this place? There was no answer for that at the moment. He tossed the saddle on the fence.

Only a short while ago he was buried in her heavenly ripe body; two hours later he was back to being a wanted fugitive on the run. Those damn Abbott brothers hadn't wasted any time getting up there. Why, he'd almost expected them to be in Dodge waiting for him when he brought the second herd up in one season, but how did they get to Nebraska so fast? He rubbed his calloused palm over his whisker-bristled mouth. There was no justice in his life. And all he could think about was the pleasures of having Glendora Brown's supple body in that bed. Damn.

22

Hailey spotted the pair of bounty hunters in the parlor. The men were seated on different couches, and each looked actively engaged with a scantily dressed whore seated on his lap. Feeling flesh and laughing freely with the girls, the two barely looked up when he came through the curtain into the room. He guessed them to be in their thirties. Dressed like cowboys, they both had on business coats, but wore silk neckerchiefs.

"So you're the pair looking for Slocum?" Hailey asked. The larger of the two men blinked his eyes and rudely moved the brunette in the pink dusty off his lap to stand up.

"Mister, do you know where he's at?"

"How much you willing to pay for him?" Hailey asked.

"Five hundred dead or alive," the big man said, by then joined by the other.

"I'm Hailey Ketchem," he said in a subdued voice. He looked around for a more private place. "Can we go outside and talk?"

"Lyle Abbott. This here is my brother, Ferd." They shook hands. Lyle told the girls they'd be back, then hitched up his pants as if uncomfortable, and the three men went out on the porch in the darkness.

"Where's Slocum?" Lyle asked the moment they were on the porch.

"First, I want to know who's paying me the reward money."

"Why, it'll come from Fort Scott. Trust me."

Hailey shook his head. "For five hundred bucks I ain't trusting a gawdamn bank. You got the cash, I'll deliver you to Slocum."

"Is he around here close?" Ferd asked.

"I'm not telling you a gawdamn thing. I can deliver him to you when you have the five hundred to pay me in cash."

The two brothers looked at each other. Hailey folded his arms on his chest and leaned back against the wall. The red light from the porch lamp bathed both men's faces while they talked back and forth under their breath.

"We can have it here in a day, maybe two. How do we know you ain't fooling us?" Lyle asked.

"You don't have to pay me if you don't get him."

"Yeah, that's right," Ferd agreed.

"How come you helping us, besides the money?" Lyle asked with a suspicious look on his face in the red light.

"He killed my brother in Dodge a couple weeks ago."

"Reason enough." Both brothers nodded in agreement.

"You sure he ain't going to run off while we're getting the money here?" Ferd asked. "We know this peckerwood. He can move out like a whiff of smoke if he gets word we're in town."

Hailey shook his head. "You boys keep low and not let the word out you're here, and he'll be here when the money arrives. I'll keep an eye on him. Hell, I've got a big stake in this too."

"I'll send a telegram for the money first thing in the morning," Lyle said.

"When you want me to check with you?"

"Two days, but don't let the sumbitch slip away."

"He won't."

"Hey, we know him. He can disappear faster than a drop of water in a drought."

"Bad son of a bitch," Ferd said under his breath.

"That's settled. Let's go back in and screw us a whore or two and celebrate," Lyle said, grabbing his crotch and making a face.

The three men laughed and filed back in the parlor. Hailey parted from the Abbotts, and went through the curtain back in the kitchen. He considered the back stairs, and then after a few seconds went up them. Those bounty men looked ordinary. Were they the only ones after Slocum? He'd expected tougher men to deal with.

At the top of the steps, he glanced back down the dark shaft. Grateful a few dim candle lamps lighted the hallway, he went to the second door.

"Whose there?" a sleep-husky voice asked in the darkness of the room.

"Hailey," he said, and began to toe off his boot.

"Well, Hailey honey, I was asleep." He saw the outline of her body getting up from the bed in the dim light. "I was really worried you wouldn't come back and play with me."

"I said I'd be back, didn't I?" he asked, impatient with her. What did she think? Stupid whore. She stood before him naked in the darkness, and he reached out and cupped her small breast.

"Oh, you like to feel things," she said, and covered his hand, holding it there.

In a few minutes, with her help, he was undressed and they were on the mattress. She smelled of lilacs, and he was growing intoxicated with the scent. On her back, she slithered down to be under where he knelt on the bed.

Her small fingers played with his emerging manhood, and his urge to stab it in her became overwhelming. He moved forward and tried to enter her. Shaking with a growing need for her, he nosed his throbbing dick into her and then drew in his breath. Too late—no way to hold it back—he felt the rush from deep in his testicles and came.

"Damn you!" he swore, and started off the bed.

"Wait!" she cried.

"Wait, hell!" he swore, and blind with anger, he began to dress. "Gawdamn you, you made me do that on purpose!"

He lashed his hand out at her. Filled with rage, he grabbed her arm and jerked her up in his face. "You no-good little whore. You made me do that on purpose."

He slapped her face back and forth. She cried out in protest. Then in a final rage, he shoved her down on the bed, anxious to be out of the room and away from that conniving slut. How did they do that to him? He used to last for hours inside a woman. What had happened to him? It was all her fault. He didn't even know when he was coming until the last moment. That made the last two times it had happened. He'd done it with that stinking squaw too. Was something wrong with his dick?

He hurried down the stairs and out the back door. The next two days he had to make damn certain Slocum didn't hightail it out of the country. They'd take shifts, he and Bret, watching Slocum. He checked his cinch, then looked back upstairs at the dark window of her room. When this matter of Slocum was over and he had his money, he'd come back and show her. He'd wear her ass out.

He put spurs to the dun. Better get that lazy Bret off that squaw of his and posted watching Slocum.

"Get up, Bret," Hailey shouted in the predawn light, standing over the bedroll containing the two of them. "You've got to get your ass down to the Brown place and make damn sure that Slocum don't ride off before we get our reward money."

"Huh?" he asked with sleep-crusted eyes.

"Get up and get dressed. We have to watch that Slocum around the clock the next two days and be damn sure he don't ride out."

"What the hell for?"

"The damn reward. Five hundred dollars. I've been work-ing on it all night, you stupid dumb-ass!"

"How the hell was I suppose to know about a damn reward for the bastard?"

"If you'd stop screwing her all the time and ride with me, you might know something!"

"Damnit, Hailey, that ain't fair at all. I do my part. You rode off and left me and that Rhodes at Sam's store."

"Both of you were too damn drunk to ride. Where's Rhodes?"

"How the hell should I know?"

"I'll find him. Get dressed and saddle your horse. We can't let Slocum slip out of our sight for the next two days." Hailey started for the house. He'd almost forgotten that Ar-nold was getting the cows that Rhodes wanted. The money sounded paltry compared to the Slocum reward, but they could use all of it. He glanced back in the faint light. Bret was up dressing.

"What you eating your brother out about?" Ma stood on the porch waiting.

"Got to be sure that Slocum don't run off for the next two days."

"Why don't we go over there and hog-tie him?"

"Ma. Let them bounty hunters get him. One dead Ketchem is enough. That Rhodes in here?"

She blocked his way. "He'll be out directly. Go out to the shed and wake Luther."

"Oh," he said, knowing full well she'd bedded the cattle buyer the night before while poor old Luther slept outside on the ground. For a moment Hailey almost grinned. Ma was turning tricks again. Even at her age, she couldn't resist making some change on her back. He wondered what she'd charged the man? One thing he did know, she would never split a penny of the money she got from Rhodes with him and Bret.

He could hear Bret cursing a horse in the pen. Good, that meant he would soon be on his way to keep an eye on

Slocum. Somehow, that man could not be allowed to slip away from them for the next two days. Back of the house, he found Luther wrapped up in a quilt on the ground.

With his boot toe, he tried to wake him. The second time he struck his toe in the man's side, the old man grunted. He was awake.

"She said get up."

"I'm coming."

"Good. I'm going to sleep a couple hours up in the shade of them cedars. You can tell that cattle buyer them cows will be ready in two days."

"Hmm, we got to put up with him that long?"

"It means money to us."

Luther made a face in the direction of the shack. That was his and her problem. Hailey didn't give a damn if she sold it or gave it away. He'd been up all night and needed some sleep.

"Just watch him?" Bret asked, ready to ride out.

"Don't let him know you're watching him either."

"I know. What if he rides off?"

"Don't let him out of your sight. He's worth five hundred in two days."

"Whew, that's a lot of money." Bret made a sign to his dour-faced squaw and then rode out.

Hailey considered for a moment giving his brother more orders, but decided that was enough. He'd relieve him later in the day. With his bedroll on his shoulder, he hiked up to where the cedars shaded the ground most of the day. There he unfurled his bedroll and went to sleep.

But all he could do was dream about coming before he could even enter a single woman. There were fat ones, skinny ones, old ones, and young ones, and each time, bang and it was over, and they always laughed at him. Then they were all naked as jaybirds in a row, and laughing so hard that some even cried at his failure. He wanted to smash them all.

He sat upright in a cold sweat. It was hot, and a strong

wind tore through the tops of the cedars. He decided it must be close to midday, and his belly growled for something to eat. Maybe Bret's squaw had something left for him to gnaw on.

Damn, his stomach felt drawn. Been over a day since he'd eaten last. He rolled up his bedding and went off to find her. In two days, he'd be a rich man and Slocum would be on his way to prison or a hanging. Good riddance to the sumbitch.

23

"Jeremy, don't look now, but there is someone up on the rim of the canyon who is spying on us," Slocum said, reining the cow ponies around to head them and the sweet-smelling rack of hay to the growing stacks near the cabin.

"Really? Who is it?"

"I'm not sure, but I've been certain for some time that someone was up there, and I finally caught sight of him."

"What're we going to do?"

"Let him stew up there for a while. Peeking on folks all day gets damn tiring. He'll get careless and show himself more as time goes on."

"Who is he?"

"Someone up to no good or too lazy to pitch hay," he said, then wiped his sweaty face on his sleeve.

"What's so funny?" Dora asked, coming with the water pail and dipper. Slocum reined up the horses, certain that they were on the opposite side of the rack from the lookout. No need to take unnecessary chances—the presence of someone on the ridge niggled him despite his comforting talk to her and the boy.

"Somebody is spying on us," Jeremy said.

"Who?" Her eyes widened.

"Don't act interested, but he's up on the rim of the canyon over there. He isn't aiming a gun or anything yet."

"Those old people we ran off?" she asked.

"It could be anyone. I don't consider him a threat so far. But he'll get tired of just sitting up there and show more of himself."

"Reckon it's the bounty hunters?" Jeremy asked.

Slocum shook his head. "No, they'd ride in if they thought I was here. And they'd for sure never show themselves. This fella is a little more lax than they are."

"Who are they? Those men after you?"

"Two brothers. They're deputy sheriffs from Fort Scott, Kansas."

"That all they do is chase you?"

"That's what a man pays them to do."

"But Slocum, can't you—" She made a face and then shook her head.

"Straighten it out? No. It happened a long time ago. Many of the witnesses are gone. A rich man's son was killed. He feels I was to blame and his pockets are obviously endless."

"But there has to be justice," she said.

"His or mine?"

"I see."

"How long can you keep getting away from these men?"

Slocum drew a deep breath. "I hope forever."

"Yes," she said softly, and then forced a smile. "I'll be along to help you two unload that."

"We can get it."

"No, Slocum. Jeremy and I have to do this ourselves when you're gone," she reminded him.

Slocum nodded, and clucked to the ponies. For an instant the image of her ripe body fitted to his filled his thoughts. Then a rock began to grow in the pit of his stomach, and a knot rose in his throat. It wouldn't be easy parting with Glendora Brown. Who was up there? Come dark he would learn his identity, or run him off if he was still there.

In late afternoon, with the last load on the stack, Slocum

felt satisfied the spy was still up in the cedars. On the back porch, he washed his hands, keeping his gaze on the ridge. He'd seen a hat once or twice. Obviously this person was not an Indian. Slowly he rubbed the lather into his calloused palms and resoaped them to take longer to study the spy's position while he had an unobstructed view of the entire ridgeline. Then he rinsed his hands, and stood under the shade of the porch and dried them on the coarse feed sack towel. It would be good to know who was up there.

He ran the edge of his sharp upper teeth over his sun-crusted lower lip. A couple of hours after dark he'd slip around and move in. The notion of someone being up there all day spying on them made him mad. Besides, whoever it was had to be up to no good, or he'd have ridden down and looked things over on some flimsy excuse. That lookout had purpose up there, and Slocum needed to know what it was for the safety of Dora and the boy.

"You hungry?" she asked from the doorway.

"Sure am."

"Good. We have more beans."

"This hay up, we need to find some meat."

"Buffalo?" Jeremy asked with excitement dancing in his eyes.

"I don't know. If we can find one."

"Where will we go to find them?" she asked.

"Up on the plains."

"We've got the hay up," Jeremy said. "Can we go soon?"

"We better go in the morning," Slocum announced, taking a place at the table.

"Take the wagon?" she asked.

"Yes, and bedrolls. May take a few days to find them."

"Great," Jeremy said, digging into his bowl of beans. "Meat would sure beat these—"

"Jeremy watch your language. The Good Lord has provided us food and we shouldn't be ungrateful."

"Yes, ma'am, but buffalo would taste a damn sight better."

She shook her head, then agreed.

"You'd have to make jerky out of most of it," Slocum said to her.

"We can do that. We'll make sausage and—I guess we have to find a buffalo first."

Slocum agreed between spoons of beans. Buffalo meat would beat beans. He could stand some fried liver too. Jeremy asked several questions about the hunt, and the three of them chattered through the meal about what they'd need to take along in the morning.

After supper, Slocum went out in the twilight and squatted on his boot heels and rolled a cigarette. In the dim light, he considered the ridge with the dark spots of stunted cedars. In another hour he planned to slip up on the spy. He turned at the rustle of Dora's dress beside him.

"He still up there?"

"I'm going to check when it gets good and dark. The moon won't come up for a couple of hours. Whoever is up there needs to do some explaining."

"Your bedroll behind the corrals?" she asked softly. "You plan to sleep there tonight?"

"Yes."

"Be careful up there," she reminded him.

"I will." He drew on the last of the cigarette, inhaled the smoke deeply, and then let it slip out. With care he ground the rest of the butt out in the dirt, never taking his gaze from the ridgeline. The soft rustle of her dress retreated to the cabin.

By starlight, Slocum checked the loads in his Colt, holstered it, and began making his way up the hillside. He used a familiar game trail, a path cut by years of buffalo and deer in their movements through the brakes to the Platte. On the rim, he made his way in the soft night wind, using the cedars for cover, and began to work his way eastward. Pausing and listening in case the spy had moved, he advanced with care.

The snort of a grazing horse made him aware he must be almost at the man's position. Squatted on his boot heels, he waited under the pungent-smelling boughs for a sign of movement. The dull clung of a metal canteen being dropped, and the soft coughing until the person cleared his throat and spat, made the lookout's position even more obvious. Slocum dropped on his belly, drew the skinning knife from his boot, and took it in his mouth. His adversary was fifty to seventy feet away in the evergreen brush. This called for some real Apache-style stealth. He shed his hat, vest, and gunbelt.

With great care he began to slither toward the lookout. The inky darkness under the cedars forced him to strain his eyes for sight of his goal. Inch by inch, he moved across the needle-strewn ground. It was a good place to discover a prairie rattler. He hoped no diamondback was in his way, but he had to be sensitive to anything and everything. By listening, he located the horse chomping grass through its bits to his right. For a few long minutes he waited in place, spread out on the dusty ground, and then when the spy cleared his throat, Slocum smiled.

His movement resumed. He was grateful for the murmur of the night wind in the tree tops to cover the sounds of his moving. Using his elbows, he slithered closer. There only appeared to be one person. But he had to be sure before he struck. One he could handle with surprise on his side. Two men, and he'd need the Colt that he'd left behind. He inched on, satisfied the throat-clearing and spitting came from only one man.

His path became blocked by a large bough. There was no way to cross it without making too much noise. With care he inched backward, and then worked his way around the bushy cedar. With the sappy smell of rosin heavy in his nose, he paused and listened again. The man was close, but Slocum needed to know which way he faced. An attack from behind would be best. He took the knife from his teeth, then wiped the beads of sweat from his upper lip.

Nothing in the inky darkness betrayed the lookout. Slocum squinted to see better. Only the small spots of stars through the branches made any light at all. Perhaps that was why Apaches never attacked at night; they couldn't see a damn thing. No, he knew they feared eternal damnation if they were killed in the darkness. Such a death for a warrior meant being excluded from heaven and walking alone in the night forever.

Then he heard the tinkle of a spur rowel to his right. He could make out the man's form, not ten feet away. The lookout rose and stood up. He stomped his boots as if his feet were asleep, and stretched his arms over his head.

Slocum rose to his feet in an instant and, the knife in his right hand, landed on the man's back, driving him to the ground. The surprise and Slocum's force flattened the burly lookout face-down.

"What the hell—"

With the blade against the skin on his neck, Slocum pinned him face-down.

"Don't move a muscle," he warned with both of his knees on the man's back. "Who are you?"

"Ketchem—Bret Ketchem."

The bank robber from Dodge? What was his business up here? Slocum eased the man's gun out of his holster and shoved it in his own belt.

"I don't have much time. You have less. Start telling me why you're up here and spying on me."

"That's our place down there."

"That's a damn lie." He pressed the knife deeper to impress Ketchem.

"No, no, they promised us that place."

"Who promised you that place?"

"I can't—Arnold did."

"Who's he?"

"Banker," the man croaked. "I'll tell you. Get that knife back."

"What did you do to deserve that place?" He shoved his

right knee deeper into the man's back for emphasis.

"We did some work for him."

"Any work you did was skullduggery. Tell me more."

"We—ah! All right, we strung up that damn Brown."

"Why?"

"For raping and killing that whore worked for him."

"He never did that." Slocum applied more pressure to the man's twisted arm.

"All right, you're hurting my arm and back. We killed the dumb slut and put her in his bed."

"Who's we?"

"Me and Hailey."

"Why are you up here?"

"Supposed to watch you."

"Why?" Slocum gave him an extra hard knee to impress him.

"Bounty hunters getting the reward money for you," he managed to say.

"When they getting it?"

"I don't know—Hailey was supposed to be up here and relieve me."

"Your brother?"

"Yeah."

"The Abbott brothers? They're the ones?"

"I guess somebody from Kansas is getting the money. What are you going to do to me?"

"Cut your balls out," Slocum said, and considered his next move.

The cooling night wind swept his sweaty face. He couldn't take Ketchem to the law in Ogallala. They were probably in on the whole deal. The banker had been in on the lynching, and no doubt the local law had been bought off. If Slocum turned Ketchem loose, he would go tell his brother and they'd be back with the Abbott brothers for him. Damn, they'd left him little choice but to turn tail and run away himself.

For the time being, he needed to keep Ketchem as a prisoner. He also needed to get Dora and the boy some meat for the winter ahead. Things grew more complicated by the hour. But at least he had proof that by Ketchem's own admission, Cy Brown had been killed by a lynch mob and it had all been a setup.

"Tell me one thing more."

"What's that?"

"Why did Arnold want Brown killed?"

"I don't know. Over a money deal, I guess. Honest, I don't know. He said we had to make it look good."

"You did that."

"Yeah, Hailey did."

"Where's he at?"

"Damned if I know. He said he'd be here to relieve me."

"Where's the Abbott brothers?"

"Ogallala, I guess."

Slocum rose up, jerked him to his feet, and drove him toward the silhouette of the horse. With Ketchem's left arm in his grasp he drove him face-first into the saddle. He reached around and took the lariat. In seconds he had Ketchem's arms tied behind his back.

"You ain't serious about cutting me, are you?" Ketchem asked in a small voice.

"I'm serious about doing something with you. I just don't know what yet." Slocum caught the horse's reins, then shoved Ketchem in the back to make him walk ahead.

He glanced at the stars. The whole thing grew more complicated by the minute. The Ketchems had planted the whore's body in Brown's bed, but they worked for Arnold. The Abbott brothers were waiting in town for a reward to pay the Ketchems. He stopped and recovered his vest and gunbelt. Then they resumed the trek to the ranch headquarters. More things were happening than he could manage to figure out.

24

Hailey woke up from his nap in late afternoon. He needed to go check on Bret. He would be getting antsy after spying on Slocum this long. But better than doing that, he should ride into Ogallala and see if the Abbott brothers were getting the money from Fort Scott to pay them. Somehow he didn't trust those two. If they thought they could get Slocum themselves and save the reward, they sure might double-cross him.

Bret would be furious if he didn't go by and relieve him, but what the hell—the money was more important. Besides, all Bret had to do was hide out up there and not let Slocum get away. While Hailey had to handle the business part of the deal.

"That damn banker promised us that Brown place, didn't he?" Ma demanded when he entered the shack. He held up his hands to silence her with Rhodes there; he didn't want to discuss the deal they'd made with Arnold. The sumbitch was already suppose to have the place put in her name.

Rhodes, seated at the table, nodded to him. "You finding out about them cows soon?"

"Yeah, I'm going into town and see about them."

"Rhodes can use a place to hold over cattle up here," she said with a pasted-on smile for the man. "He says if we can get that Brown place back, he'll work with us on it.''

"We'll get it back," Hailey muttered, and dipped some stew out of the boiling kettle on the stove. Where had she put Luther while she entertained Rhodes? It was none of his concern, but he knew the old man wasn't happy with the cattle buyer moving in and rutting her. Damn. He sat down and considered the steaming stew. He had to talk to Arnold about the cow deal. Better mention the Brown place again and how they were supposed to be getting title to it too. Remind Arnold of what he'd promised, and then see those Abbott brothers. So they didn't double-cross him.

"You going to spell your brother?" she asked, pouring him some coffee.

"Not yet. I got to ride to town and find out something. I'll come back by and do that."

"If you could talk Injun you could send that black-eyed thing over there." Ma nodded toward the outside.

"He don't need no distraction watching Slocum."

"Yeah, you're right," she said, and sat down on Rhodes's lap. "I been distracting you?"

The cow buyer laughed and hugged her in his arms. "Yeah, you been doing it regular like."

Ma might be getting gray-headed, but she still knew how to work a man. Like the old days, when he and Bret took turns peeking through the cracks in the wall at her and some old boy banging away at it in the bed. Why, some of them had been hung bigger than his paint horse.

He burned his mouth on the spoonful of hot stew, and then chased it down with scalding coffee from the tin cup that seared his lip. Damn—water squirted from his eyes. He bolted to his feet and gasped for breath.

"You all right?" she asked.

"Yeah," he managed. "Hotter than hell."

If he hadn't been so lost in thought about times past, he would have been more careful. He sat down, and almost overturned the bench.

"You going to be all right?" she asked.

"Yeah. I was thinking about that reward business."

"That's going to be real nice," she said, and patted Rhodes on the face.

"Get rid of that damn Slocum too," Rhodes grumbled.

"Right," Hailey agreed.

How old was Rhodes? Maybe forty? He had lots of gray hair. Ma had to be past fifty. Maybe folks didn't ever stop doing it. Carefully he sampled the next spoon of stew. It was cool enough, but still, his mouth felt on fire and he could hardly taste the food.

Damn, Rhodes didn't have to feel her up with him looking on. He didn't know why, but it made him anxious. Like spying on her years before had made him feel guilty, but he'd still done it. She'd known they'd watched her, too. She'd hinted around that she was proud of doing it and of them seeing it.

He couldn't eat anything else; his mouth hurt too bad. Standing up, he excused himself. Rhodes and Ma were so busy kissing and getting worked up they didn't care. He slapped on his hat and started out the door.

"What should I tell Bret if he comes back?" Ma asked.

"Tell him to go back up there and keep his damn eye on Slocum. We can't afford to lose him now."

"I will," she said, and let out a loud squeal. He knew what that meant; Rhodes had his hand up under her damn dress. Hailey shook his head in disbelief, and went to saddle the paint by starlight.

"When's that bastard up at the house going to leave?" Luther asked, quietly coming up to him.

"Couple of days."

"Can't be too soon."

"We'll make some good money off of him," he said to reassure the man. No sense in old Luther going off half cocked about Rhodes sleeping with her—they could use the cow trade money too.

"Damn her—I can see her acting nice to him—"

"Luther, go sleep in the saddle shed and forget it for now."

"Yeah, yeah," he muttered, and went off.

Hailey mounted up and rode for town. The stars were dim when he reached the ferry. He paid the man and led the spooky paint on the rickety barge.

"Been anyone come over tonight?"

"A drummer in a buggy headed for town," the ferryman said.

"Ain't seen two fellas in suits and cowboy hats?"

"Them bounty hunters?"

"You know them?"

"Yeah, they came through here two days ago asking me more questions than I could answer. Said they'd pay me good if I saw this Slocum fella and I let them know."

"You seen him?" Hailey asked. Under the light of the small lantern, he watched the man's face carefully.

"Hell, from their description of him, he could have been anyone of a dozen fellas crossed here in the past week." Hailey nodded, relieved the man didn't know any more than that about Slocum.

He rode around town to the banker's place first. Arnold came out in the dark at his knock.

"You make the cow deal?" Hailey asked.

"Yes. two days—that'll be Thursday—he can ride out to the Laughtin place and get the cattle. I'll be there at ten o'clock. Don't pay them. I'll collect the money, and don't discuss the price with them either. It's seven bucks a head to them period is all they need to know."

"How do we split it?"

"You get fifty cents."

"No," Hailey said, feeling confident. "We each get a buck and a half per head and you get your mortgage money."

"I'm not going to argue. Fine."

"Ma is worried you ain't fixed that land deal up for her and Luther to get that Brown place."

"I can't now that that woman is here. Brown never would give me a mortgage on it."

"Then make up one. Ma ain't happy at that shack of ours."

"Tell her to be patient."

"She ain't a patient person, you know that."

In the light coming through the kitchen window Hailey watched Arnold bob his head. "I'll get it fixed when the time is right. This Mrs. Brown has no means of support. She'll have to leave soon. Tell your ma to rest easy."

"Thursday at the Laughtin place. The cow buyer will be there."

"Right. Lacy said a wanted poster out of Kansas arrived on his desk for you two."

"You tell him to burn it?"

"Yeah, but—"

"He better burn it he knows what's good for him."

"Let me handle Lacy," Arnold insisted. "You three keep out of sight until it blows over."

"Arlie's dead."

"Damn, I wondered why the reward was only for the two of you."

"I got business. You get that land taken care of for Ma."

"I can't do—"

"Hey, that was our deal."

"I'll handle it when the Brown woman is gone."

"She'll be gone in a day or so."

"Fine," Arnold said, sounding huffy.

"Thursday, we'll be there for them cows," Hailey said, and left the porch for his horse at the back of the yard. Arnold never answered him, but Hailey didn't care—three hundred from the cattle deal and five from Slocum's reward. They'd be rich as hell. Time to go check on the Abbott brothers.

Old Eck at the stables sent him to find them at Willard's pool hall. When he stepped in the back door he spotted, through the curtain of smoke, Lyle bent over the table to make a shot. Good, they were still in town. Maybe he was wrong about them double-crossing him. Of course, they didn't know where Slocum was and he did. They'd obviously been on his trail for some time and wanted him caught badly.

Lyle looked up mildly at him and nodded. Ferd did the same from where he chalked his cue at the side.

"Any word about the reward?" Hailey asked under his breath.

"Be here Thursday," Lyle said, then made the shot and the white cue ball sped off to click on target. The seven ball looked destined for the far corner pocket, but at the last second banked off the side and spun on the green felt.

"Shame you missed that," Ferd said, and stepped in to put away the twelve.

"Meet you mid-afternoon Thursday at the stables," Hailey said, checking around to make sure that no one in the place had an eye on him. That news about the Kansas wanted posters wasn't good.

Lyle looked up, ready to shoot again after his brother missed his. "You better have him. We ain't paying for thin air."

"I'll have him by the balls."

"Good." Lyle sunk the seven ball.

25

"If you make one peep, I am going to gag you," Slocum said, then forced his prisoner to sit down with his back to the cedar tree.

"You ain't leaving me out here alone?"

"I'll be back come daylight."

"But there's coyotes out here—"

"You better hope they ain't hungry," he said, and finished tying the man securely to the tree.

"Damn you, Slocum."

"Better save your breath for the jury that's going to want to hang you and your brother."

"Who's going to believe you?"

"The real law."

"Ha."

Slocum led Ketchem's horse to the corral, and turned when he heard soft footsteps. He could see it was Dora running towards him.

"You find that horse up there?" she whispered.

"It belongs to Bret Ketchem."

"Where is he?"

"Tied up to that tree where they butchered cattle."

"Can he get away?" she asked.

He stripped the saddle and pad off, then turned the horse

into the lot. "No, he's there until we need him."

"What are you going to do next?"

"Find some real law and have him and his brother tried for murdering your husband."

"He wasn't guilty after all?"

"Not guilty of murdering that woman."

"How can we prove it?"

"That may prove hard. We've got Ketchem's confession, and the law in Ogallala is liable to be in cahoots with the banker who hired them."

"Oh, it gets worse."

"I figure your husband knew something about the banker or was blackmailing him."

"Really? Oh, Slocum, what can we do?"

"If I had all that down at the moment, I'd start out and settle it."

"Where do we start?"

"Make certain Bret doesn't get free and no one comes to his aid."

"What are you going to do?"

"There's one chance that I can scare the local law into taking action to save their own neck. He may have just looked the other way long enough. In that case he will have to act or be implicated."

"But the Abbott brothers are in town."

"I'm not going looking for them."

"But what if they—"

"I'll cross that bridge when I get there. You and Jeremy watch out. Someone is coming to relieve Bret Ketchem. And don't you two get hurt."

"Wait. We can put the prisoner in the wagon. Jeremy and I can take you to town in the wagon too and they won't see you."

"That might work. Let's hitch up the rig." Her idea sounded better than anything he could think of. Tie his bay to the tailgate so he had a way out, just in case—that would be better than leaving her to wait for Ketchem's replacement to come.

"I'll get Jeremy up," she said. "He won't want to miss this."

"Dora?"

"Yes," she said, and turned. He took her in his arms and kissed her hard on the mouth, savoring her ripe body pressed to his. This might be his last time to hold her. He didn't want to think about it. They parted at last. He licked the honey from his lips and watched her run off to the house.

Ketchem was gagged and forced to lie face-down in the alfalfa-smelling wagon. Slocum pulled the tarp over himself and Ketchem when she drove up to the ferry.

Jeremy jumped down and ran ahead to ring the bell. At last a sleepy-sounding man came out of the shack with a lantern.

"What's the matter, can't you wait till morning?"

"No, we've got to make a stage."

"Hell's bells—sorry, ma'am—but it's two bits extra this late."

"We'll pay it," she said, and kicked the brake off with her foot. Slocum could feel her driving the mules onto the deck of the barge. The team shifted around once on the vessel. She climbed down and told Jeremy to hold the right mule, she'd get the left one.

The creaking of the crank began, and the man grumbled about no sleep. The Platte's current slapped against the side of the ferry. Soon they struck the north dock with a bang. At last, he heard her climb on the seat, and Jeremy joined her. A good lurch, and the mules were off.

A safe distance from the ferry, she called out to him.

"What next?" she asked.

"We've got to find the sheriff and I'd bet he's in bed."

"Go by the jail first?"

"Good idea. It's up the main street."

Slocum sat up. No one would recognize him in the darkness with the wagon box sides to hide him. What if his scheme didn't work? Then he might have put her and the boy in jeopardy. He drew a deep breath. Something had to work.

She paused before the dark jail, and Jeremy went and rapped on the door. Slocum got on his knees and undid the leather thong on his Colt. He watched over the edge of the wagon. A light came on and someone shouted, "Hold you dang horses."

"Sheriff?"

"Yeah, who's asking?" He blinked his eyes against the darkness.

"I am," Slocum said aloud, and grasped Ketchem by the arm. He dragged the protesting man out after himself. "I've got a killer for you."

"A what?"

"Let's get inside and talk," Slocum said, and shoved Ketchem in the door ahead of him.

"Why, that's Bret Ketchem. Who's he killed, mister?"

"Cy Brown and a whore who worked for him."

"He did what?"

"Him and his brother murdered a girl and put her body in Brown's bed. Next they formed a lynch mob, then they hung Brown."

"But why?"

Slocum undid the gag on Ketchem. "You tell him why."

"It's all a lie," Ketchem gasped for his air. "I never—"

"What did you get out of it?" the sheriff demanded.

"A hundred bucks, and we were supposed to get his farm too."

Slocum nodded in satisfaction at Dora and Jeremy. The lawman had taken the bait. No matter what the sheriff's involvement had been, Ketchem had confessed.

"Tell him who hired you," Slocum went on to Ketchem.

"Arnold."

"Arnold, my God, man, that's the—"

"Sheriff, this is Cy Brown's wife and her son, Jeremy, from Texas."

"Well, ma'am, I'm sorry, but things are happening so damn fast around here. I better untie Ketchem and put him in a cell."

"Isn't Arnold's son a deputy?" Slocum asked.

"Yeah, he is. But that doesn't matter. He wasn't part of the deal, was he?" the sheriff asked Ketchem.

"Ha, he's the one left the jail unlocked for us."

"You have any other deputies you can call on?" Slocum asked.

"Well, I can't go arrest the biggest businessman in town in the middle of the night—"

"Better do it before he figures out the deal went sour."

"You're right. By the way, who are you?"

"Folks call me Slocum."

"Lacy Dutton. Well, Deputy Slocum, grab a Greener off that rack and we'll go arrest the Arnolds. I may never have another job in this town nor a loan, but I guess it's my duty, isn't it?"

"I'd say so." Slocum broke open the shotgun and loaded it with two brass shells. He turned to Dora and the boy while Dutton jailed Ketchem. "You and Jeremy stay inside the jail and don't let anyone in until we get back."

"Hate to leave a woman to guard a murderer," Dutton said, putting on his hat.

"Sheriff, no one's coming or going from this jail until you return," Dora promised him.

"Yes, ma'am."

Dutton and Slocum walked the half block in silence. Only the creak of the boardwalk under their feet or the distant barking of a dog broke the night's quiet.

"Beautiful woman, that Mrs. Brown," Dutton said, sounding impressed.

"Yes, she is. Shame she's a widow."

"Guess you and her . . ."

"No, sir, we are just good friends."

"Hmmm. If I was ten years younger . . ."

"Why, Sheriff, I don't think there's that much difference in your ages."

"I'll be forty-two in the fall."

"Why, that ain't old at all."

Slocum noticed the new spring in the lawman's steps. They crossed the street and went the last two blocks through a residential area. The big two-story house loomed in the night against the sky. In the starlight they approached it, walking up the center of the street.

"You know if I'm wrong—"

"You aren't."

"Whew, it's going to take lots of nerve to arrest the two of them."

"They were in on the lynching."

"But a low-down criminal's words against the most influential man in the county?"

"It's your call."

"I know." Dutton bobbed his head. "Let's get this over with."

"Yes, sir."

The sleepy banker and his irate son were taken into custody without incident. They were marched back to the jail amid their verbal threats about their lawyer and charges of false arrest. Locked in the jail cell next to Ketchem, the senior Arnold ignored him, while the younger one threatened to kill him for lying.

"I ain't lying," Ketchem shouted. "Arnold needed Brown's money to cover his losses at the bank."

Dutton turned and blinked his eyes in disbelief at the prisoners in the cells.

Slocum nodded at Dora. They had the answer. He'd wondered where the man's fortune had gone—now they knew.

"You leaving?" Dutton asked.

"Have to get back and do our chores at the ranch," she said to him.

"Mrs. Brown. When I get this matter of your husband's

murder settled, could I come by and, say, have some tea with you one day?''

"Sheriff Dutton, Jeremy and I would be glad to have you come by anytime. Wouldn't we?''

"Yes, sir.''

"There's one more in this deal,'' Slocum reminded Dutton.

"I know. Hailey Ketchem. I'll get him before sundown.''

"Yes, and the old woman and man had a hand in it somewhere.''

"I'll check that out. Slocum, you ever need a job?''

"Thanks.'' They shook hands and parted.

From the back of the wagon, Slocum drew out his saddle and bedroll, then tossed them on the bay horse. It would be light in another hour.

"You're coming by for the roan, aren't you?'' she asked.

"No, I better ride on. Save you more trouble.'' He dug in his pants pocket and took out three twenty-dollar gold pieces. "Buy a fat beef and supplies. I'll drop by and see how you are doing one day. Jeremy, you can have the roan.''

"I can't take this money,'' she protested.

"Yes, you can.''

"No, Slocum, it isn't right.''

"Dora, I won't ever forget you. So take it. I have more.''

"Where will you go?''

"I need to see about the other brother. Then clear out of the country.''

"Be careful,'' she said. Then she threw her arms around him.

He had to leave her; the knot in his throat was choking him. She finally let go, looking downcast, and then said good-bye. He shook Jeremy's hand. "Sorry about the buffalo hunt. Maybe another time.''

The boy understood. For his age he'd done a lot of growing up since he'd left Texas. Slocum mounted and waved to them and Dutton on the porch. Then he rode off.

26

"Where in the hell's that damn Bret gone off to?" Hailey asked aloud. Couldn't trust him to simply spy on Slocum. No, he was off and gone somewhere. Hailey gritted his teeth. When he found him, he would crown him with a stick of stove wood.

In the first pink of dawn, Hailey stood on top of the canyon and peered down into the darkness that hid the Brown homestead. No sign of his brother anywhere on the ridge. He booted his horse downhill on the trail. Perhaps Slocum had run off and Bret was on his trail. No telling about Bret. And Hailey had never seen this woman that Ma kept harping about. Probably be as ugly as hell. He reined up his paint and listened. They must not have a dog; he had not heard one bark.

He dismounted behind the shed and came ahead on foot. He blinked in disbelief at the saddle on the fence. His brother's kack. The bay he discovered in the corral. The animal had belonged to Jennings. He hurriedly crossed to the house, pistol in hand, then lifted the latch and shoved open the door.

No one inside, he decided after a quick inspection. Where had they gone? There were wagon tracks everywhere in the yard. They must have hauled in the fresh-smelling hay. But where were Bret and Slocum? Damn, he didn't have time to run everything down.

"Bret! Bret!" he shouted through his hands. Then he listened for an answer. Nothing, no answer. Only a few mourning doves cooed. It was spooky that no one was about the place. In his tight-fitting boots, he half ran for the back of the shed and gathered his horse. Something funny had happened here. He didn't know what, but Bret wasn't there and his horse and gear were. Had they captured his brother? They couldn't take Bret to town. Maybe *she* could, but Slocum wouldn't dare show his face there—he'd get arrested. Hailey booted the horse for the ferry. The operator would know if they had captured Bret and taken him to town.

His horse lathered and out of wind, he drew up at the ferry dock. The barge was on the north bank letting off a rig, and he'd have to wait for its return. Damn, everything took time and he had so little. Bret might talk under pressure—then Hailey would sure have to hightail it out of the country. With Slocum missing, he couldn't collect the reward from those brothers, the Abbotts.

At last he heard the squeal of the winch being wound up, and the ferry headed back across. It took forever, and the man operating it looked in no hurry.

"You seen my brother Bret?" he shouted before the man even docked it.

The man shook his head with a blank look.

"Someone came through here with a wagon and mules?" Hailey asked.

"That was late last night. Woke me up to go catch a stage."

"Who was it?"

"Some woman and a boy—I never caught their name. That boy told me the other day he lived on the Brown place."

"That's them. You sure there wasn't someone else in that wagon?"

"Damned if I know. She's the one paid me. I never seen nobody else."

"What time was that?"

"Midnight, I guess."

"What stage were they taking?"

"Goldurned if I know of a stage goes out at that time."

"Shit. Dead or alive, my brother had to be in that wagon."

"I never seen him."

"Take me across. I've got to find out what she's up to. Let's go."

He paid the man his fare on the far side of the river, then leaped his horse off the ferry before it docked and fanned him for Ogallala.

Slocum saw the rider coming and reined off behind some freight wagons. He watched Hailey ride past at a full gallop.

"That man's in a helluva hurry," one of the teamsters said, taking the cob pipe out of his mouth.

"He sure is—to go to jail," Slocum said with a grin, and booted the bay out in the road again. He twisted in the saddle and studied the man's back. Hailey Ketchem was riding right into the arms of the law. Sheriff Lacy Dutton would be waiting for him. Satisfied the matter was settled for Glendora Brown, Slocum short-loped for the river.

It was late afternoon, and far to the south of the Platte, when he caught up with the Gypsies and their brightly colored vans. The sound of harness bells on their high-stepping horses and the strains of a squeeze organ accompanied them. Men and women both wore colorful costumes of bright red and yellow silk. Children streaming bright veils in the wind ran alongside.

A dark-eyed woman on a long-necked horse rode out and joined him. Her low-cut blouse exposed her olive-colored cleavage, and her horsemanship showed well.

"Going far?" she asked.

"They tell me the end of the world is out there somewhere,'' Slocum said, and waved to the southwest.

"Will you jump off the edge when you find it?"

"Depends what's down there," he said.

She laughed. "Good. I will ride along and see what you jump for."

"It would have to be good."

"Oh, yes," she said, and drew up straight in the saddle. She possessed an exquisite body, he decided when she threw her chest out and then looked at him out of the coal-black eyes. *Yes, I see you.*

Besides the edge of the world, Colorado was out there too, only a short ways to the line.

Five days later, Slocum rode in from La Junta and bought the latest Omaha paper. He found her seated on a blanket beside the stream where they were camped, waiting for him.

He dismounted, left the bay ground-tied, and straightened the paper to read the front-page story.

"Ogallala Banker Indicted in Lynching," the headline said. Other area men were also arrested. Jeremiah Arnold, president of the Platte River Bank, had been charged with inciting a riot and planning the vigilante-style murder of Cy Brown. Also indicted were Hailey and Bret Ketchem, and an area storekeeper, Sam Grove, who helped them frame and then murder Brown under the pretext of vigilante actions. Also charged as an accessory in the crime was Arnold's son Joe, a deputy sheriff at the time.

According to Sheriff Lacy Dutton, as soon as the lawyers could settle the amount in question, Brown's widow would be reimbursed for her late husband's losses.

"What did you learn?" Agatha asked, pouring a glass of wine for Slocum. In the shade of the sparse cottonwoods, the prairie wind swept the raven-black hair into her face. She pushed the hair aside and held it back with her jeweled fingers.

"Justice is being served in Nebraska," he said, satisfied.

"Ha. Let's play cards some more. You have won too much of my money." She dropped to her knees, then sat on the blanket with her shapely calves exposed, shuffling the cards.

He agreed, seated cross-legged across from her on other side of the blanket. She already owed him twelve bucks— at a dollar, well, maybe two dollars a night for her to sleep with him, he'd be almost a whole week with her trading her steamy services on the debt. Slocum smiled and drew in a deep breath of the hot dry air, thinking about Glendora Brown. She was a hard one to forget. He closed his eyes, then picked up his hand and inspected the cards. Three queens, two eights. At this rate he would be over a week getting his money back from this woman.